Myshka's Shawl

Myshka's Shawl

Anne Nelson

Copyright © 2011 by Anne Nelson.

Library of Congress Control Number: 2011916147
ISBN: Hardcover   978-1-4653-6307-7
              Softcover   978-1-4653-6306-0
              Ebook   978-1-4653-6308-4

All rights reserved. No part of this book may be reproduced or transmitted in any form or by any means, electronic or mechanical, including photocopying, recording, or by any information storage and retrieval system, without permission in writing from the copyright owner.

This is a work of fiction. Names, characters, places and incidents either are the product of the author's imagination or are used fictitiously, and any resemblance to any actual persons, living or dead, events, or locales is entirely coincidental.

This book was printed in the United States of America.

To order additional copies of this book, contact:
Xlibris Corporation
1-888-795-4274
www.Xlibris.com
Orders@Xlibris.com

Dedicated

to

Michaela

Acknowledgements

Sheila Watkins
Zoë Wakelin-King
Jennifer Allen and
Radana Metson

Thank you my friends, for giving me the encouragement I needed to believe in my writing.

Thanks also to Jen Hiuser, my editor.

And last but not least to my husband, Bob, who is always there for me.

Prologue 1986-1989

Czechoslovakia, September 1986

Her name was Michaela Velkovskova, but they called her Myshka, "Little Mouse". She was three years old, quick and bright and curious and she loved her Daddy. They arrived at her Uncle Dalibor's house on a rain-filled night. They were dishevelled, wet and tired. Dalibor settled them by the fire and offered the child warm milk and honey. She took the cup in her tiny hands, her face registering distaste at the first sip, but she drank it anyway.

In the way of small children she appeared accepting of the loss of her mother, but if she were to lose her father as well it would be a cruel act to inflict upon one's daughter. Dalibor Velkovsky told his brother Zdenek so after they had put the child to bed. He failed to convince him however, that a life in Canada with new parents would not be the best thing a father could do for his daughter, especially under the present threat.

Zdenek was adamant and plans went ahead and all in all Dalibor had never been so relieved as when the dangerous arrangement went off without a hitch. By September of 1986, his brother and niece both landed safely in Canada. A month later, Dalibor himself had been instrumental in the safe return of his brother into his home country across the border from neighbouring Austria.

"Why did you not stay in Canada?" he asked him. "Why would you leave your precious daughter in the hands of strangers?" To his astonishment, Zdenek became tearful.

"I ask myself the same question," he said. "Myshka became withdrawn when we arrived in Toronto. She would not eat properly, but the couple that were to transfer her to a family for adoption tried to convince me she would be all right. Throughout my journey home I realised more and more that the sum of money they received from us was their main reason for taking her. They promised to keep me informed, which reassured me to some extent. But I admit that I keep seeing her little face on the day I left. I could not bear to tell her I would not be returning."

"You've got to return," Dalibor told him. "You can't do this to your dead wife or your little daughter!"

"I know!"

But the terrible truth was that the Secret Police were waiting for Zdenek on his return to his home in Bohemia. A week or two after Zdenek's arrest, a letter was smuggled through from Vienna and handed to Dalibor. It said that Michaela was safe and had been officially adopted by an established family in Toronto, and that she would soon receive Canadian citizenship. She would then be able to begin a new life with a new name. There were no details. There was no return address. Dalibor read it with a sinking heart. Poor little girl. Could she be happy now? It felt as if Michaela's existence had been eliminated. What could he do? He had always been extremely careful, knowing that he was watched because of his brother's activities which had been much more overt than his own. Now, with his brother in captivity and his niece lost, he wondered what options he had. Should he now take the route he had sent so many on before him? Should he go to Canada and find out if his niece was really in good hands? He pondered for a long time, then took pen and paper and sat down to write a coded letter to his partner-in-collaboration, Jan Smid. He had made his decision.

Dalibor escaped safely from Czechoslovakia into Austria on November 10th, 1986, and went on to Jan's sister Jana, at the address in Vienna. He was put in touch with the office that had facilitated his brother's entry into Canada. Here, he found less help than he had hoped for.

"Why can you not tell me the name and address of these people who took our little girl?" he stormed.

They had quite a time quietening him down. They reminded him of the sensitivity of the situation. These were difficult times for everyone. They did not want to cause trouble.

Dalibor was incensed: "I do not want to get anyone into trouble. I just want to trace my niece."

"Then why did your family put us to the trouble of getting her into Canada?" one of them demanded. A terrible thought dawned on Dalibor.

"Are you telling me that she went into Canada illegally?" His voice rose in panic. The man's lips lifted in a slight sneer but he did not answer. Dalibor thought quickly. He must tread carefully.

"I'm sorry," he said. "You must understand that she is my brother's child. Now that my brother has disappeared into our bottomless system, I am concerned about his little girl." Supercilious eyebrows were raised.

"She is perfectly safe now." Dalibor kept his temper with difficulty.

"I mean that I personally want to know exactly *how* safe."

"Where are you staying in Vienna?" Dalibor gave the address without thinking.

"Wait there until we contact you. That's the best we can do for now."

Dalibor left unhappy. He was, if anything, more worried. These people were not as he had imagined. They did not have the zeal and patriotism to which he was accustomed. He did not go straight back to Jana's home but walked the streets for almost an hour. He was distressed. Something was not right. He phoned Jana and quickly asked if Jan had arrived. She answered him in German which he thought strange, but being prepared for danger at all times, he listened without comment to what she said.

"Hallo Frieda!" were her first words. Then after the briefest of pauses. "Ja, ja. Ist gut. Bis spaeter, na? Wiederhoeren." And she immediately replaced the receiver.

Something must be dreadfully wrong. She had called him "Frieda" and inferred that she would speak to him later. He decided immediately that he would not return to his lodging. Hopping onto a city tram he rode through several stops, disembarked and jumped onto another tram travelling across town. Eventually he felt lost enough to be able to look for a cheap hotel and lie low for a while. He would try phoning Jan later.

Dalibor found a modest gasthof in the Simmering district. In the draughty little room he flung his backpack on the floor, lay on the bed and slept. When he awoke it was already dark. Along the corridor outside his bedroom was a bathroom, where he showered even though the water was cool.

He went down in search of food, in the small, friendly pub-restaurant similar to those in his own country except for the higher prices, but he ate well and then went out to phone Jan. This time Jan answered. As by agreement, Jan simply spoke a number when he heard his name spoken by Dalibor:

"Seven!" Jan hung up. Dali checked his list and found "seven" to be the name of a metro station. He looked at his subway map and saw that it was a good way from where Jan lived but not so far from his own new lodgings, so he decided to walk.

His way lay along the Simmering Strasse towards the center of the city. The night was fine and dry and Vienna sparkled in the dark, as his own beloved cities did not. The walk cleared his head but did not raise his hopes.

The rendezvous was to be near the main ticket office of the small station. Dalibor had never actually had to do this before. He had never been out of Czechoslovakia for that matter. But he knew the drill. They all did.

He arrived first and bought a newspaper, rather than scrutinise all the passengers coming up the escalators. Jan arrived shortly and they fell into step, heading for the nearest bar. Jan took a good look around to make sure they weren't being followed. Once settled with a beer, Jan said,

"Something's gone wrong. What did you say to get them all suspicious?" Dali's eyebrows shot up.

"I said I wanted to know where Michaela was."

"You must have said more than that," Jan accused flatly.

"Well yeah! I realised that they had entered Myshka into Canada illegally. And told them so." Jan drew a deep breath and looked thoughtful.

"Mm! Is that all? Are you sure?"

"I think so. Are those guys on the up and up? I mean what is wrong with me wanting to know how to get in touch with my niece?"

"I'm not sure. There is something fishy going on. They were at my place this afternoon looking for you. That has me worried."

"Who?"

"People we normally trust."

"What do you think is going on?"

"I think we can still trust them. But these people you saw earlier about Michaela's whereabouts have some doubts about you."

"You know I can be trusted, Jan. What's going on?"

"Tell me exactly what was said at your meeting today." Dalibor went over it again, trying to be as exact as possible. At last Jan began to understand.

"I suspect that this particular bunch is doing a bit of business on the side. Trouble is you can never tell who is hand in glove with whom in this game. I'll go back and smooth the waters and we'll meet again tomorrow, before I return home. I hope, in God's name, we will meet again."

"I'm pretty sure we will. Don't worry. And let's hope you can make some sense out of this for me. Thanks friend!"

"I'll do my best. Where are you staying?"

"In a small hotel about a kilometre from here. I changed my address after the call to your sister today." Jan grinned.

"This is how we live, eh? Even here in the so called free world." Jan did not ask Dalibor's new address. The environment in which they had grown up bred secrecy in their mothers' milk.

It turned out that Zdenek's arrangements for Michaela had indeed been separate from the usual business done by the excellent group helping refugees escape from the communist bloc countries. Normally legal help was given for entrance into Canada and other countries, but the process was often long and tedious with many delays. Zdenek had neither the time nor the money and had thus succumbed to hastier channels. Coming as he did from a country where to break the law was a way of redemption rather than a crime, perhaps he had not realised the implications of having the same attitude in a western country. Dalibor cursed loudly and fluently at his brother's lack of foresight once he grasped the truth of the situation. Michaela had somehow evaded the system. Now she was a Canadian citizen by default and Dalibor did not know how to trace her.

The most expedient plan was to go the same route. Maybe, for a sum, he could trace the couple in Toronto that had handed Michaela on, although he was reluctant to do this. Preferably, he could throw himself on the mercy of Austria, the normal procedure, and receive permission to stay in Vienna. As a refugee himself, he could become a free agent. But all this would take time and he felt the need for speed every time he thought of little Myshka. He cursed again, helplessly, at his failure to have convinced Zdenek.

Another interview was arranged. This time the office seemed sympathetic. They had had time to review his case. They said that they expected one more letter from the family in Ontario where the child was living, and that they would in fact allow him to send off a letter to the family expressing his wish to know about her and why. This pacified Dalibor a little. At least it was something while he waited for asylum to be granted. He would then apply to go to Canada himself. If he established connection with the family, he could see for himself how she was keeping and be there for her; be a real uncle to her.

He applied to the Austrian authorities for asylum and set about learning English while he waited for all the red tape.

Of course, the letter he wrote to Michaela never arrived. Dalibor guessed bitterly that it had never been sent. Nor did he ever hear from the family. "The least known the better," was the usual motto. Dalibor doubted that Michaela's new Canadian family would ever know Michaela's background, or about the uncle who sought to keep a loving connection with her.

Months later, still living in Vienna, now with a job to help pay his way, he concentrated on saving every groschen he could. He worked as foreman in a shoe factory; a job his fluent German qualified him to do. In his own country he had taught mathematics at the gymnasium in Novy Jicin.

At one time he visited the office where he had first been interviewed, but found no trace of it ever having existed. Jan had returned to Czechoslovakia and there could be no safe contact with his past associates now. He was on his own.

It was May of 1988 when he was finally able to travel to Toronto. Almost two years had gone by. His English was poor from lack of practice, but he managed to locate the offices which dealt officially with adoptions. Of course, in their books there was no record of a Michaela Velkovsky being put up for adoption anywhere. They were very sympathetic. They gave him lists of societies to phone. He looked so pathetic and lost that they assigned him a young woman to assist him with the telephone calls. Her name was Beth Smythe and for a few hours that afternoon, right there in the office, she called the numbers he had been given. They had no success. Then Beth suggested that as a refugee, especially a possible illegal entry, Michaela might not have been entered under her own name. She may not have had a birth certificate. They narrowed the search down to two possibilities for 1986: two children that had been found without documents, both given the name Mary. Dalibor grew very excited and asked for their particulars. Beth found the records of both girls. There was a photograph of each of them. One of them was only a small baby. The second child, perhaps three years old and unable to speak, was apparently mentally challenged. She had been found wandering in a local park, had been taken into care and then adopted. Her records showed her new name, Mary Morton, and a blurred photograph of a thin dark wan girl with a vacant look. Dalibor asked the meaning of "mentally challenged".

"This is not our Myshka!" he stated, dismissing the picture. Beth suggested that she find the child, but Dalibor vehemently denied that this could possibly be his little niece. And besides, he had received a letter saying that she had been adopted into a family in Toronto. It had not said that she had been abandoned.

The journey had been deeply disappointing, but Dalibor was grateful for Beth's efforts. She in turn was sorry that they had failed to find Myshka, and she promised herself and him that she would not forget the Little Mouse.

The following year, in 1989, the people of Czechoslovakia won their freedom in an amazing peace rally held in Wenceslas Square in Prague. Dalibor Velkovsky returned to reunite with his family and help his country celebrate. This was some consolation at least. But the memory of Myshka still lay heavily in his heart.

Toronto, September 1986

Ladislav and Dora Andrasky struggled. The little girl refused to eat. She cried all the time and the only word she spoke was "Tati", which, Ladislav explained to Dora, meant "Daddy," in the Czech language.

Dora was increasingly worried and also sad. She was fond of children and had enjoyed caring for the little ones she had so far received from this dubious agency that her refugee husband had joined. She had rationalized that it must be all right, really, because the new parents were always ecstatically happy with their babies, and the babies were desperately in need of parents. This made her less unhappy to give them up when their time came. But Michaela was proving to be a challenge.

At three years old, she was not a baby. Her adoptive parents were in Alberta, and would not be able to collect her for another two weeks.

"What are we going to do, Ladya?" she begged for the umteenth time. "She'll starve if we can't get something into her soon."

"Give her water. Make her drink it."

"I won't force her. She's frightened enough."

"Then there is nothing to do." And Ladislav left, grabbing his coat and slamming the door behind him.

Dora set the child on her knee.

"Come on little girl! Eat up! It'll make you feel better." But Michaela stared disconsolately at Dora as tears trickled down her cheeks and chin. Her little pink tongue crept out to catch a few drops. Dora almost wept.

Michaela fell asleep in her arms and Dora carried her to bed. The child felt feverish and Dora's fears grew. When Ladya returned with a six-pack of beer and a bottle of plum brandy, Dora told him that Michaela had a fever. He scowled and cursed a little in his own language, but Dora knew he was only expressing his worry. She waited till he'd drunk a couple of beers and then approached the subject again, laying out the plan that had been forming in her mind.

"If she's not better in the morning, why don't we wrap her up good, bring her to the park, and then phone the police? We won't get into trouble that way, and they'll be able to help the poor kid."

Ladislav stared in shocked amazement. She remained silent.

"What do I tell to the boss?"

"Just tell him she's sick and going to die. She hasn't eaten or drunk for nearly three days. She's getting dehydrated." It was Ladislav's turn for silence. He got up and went to the phone. A dialogue ensued in Czech that sounded to Dora's ears like a gutteral chirping of birds. She jumped when he slammed down the receiver.

"Get rid of her. They said to get rid of her." And Ladislav went to bed, taking the plum brandy with him.

In the morning, Michaela had worsened, almost to the point of delirium. They wrapped her up warmly in her shawl and a blanket, and set off to the park. It was about eight thirty, too early for the children and their carers and too busy for anyone to notice a couple with a child in a park. They set her down near the sand pit in the shadow of the big climbing frame, which would hide her from eyes in the windows adjacent to the park. Then as calmly as possible, keeping to the trees, they left and headed for a telephone call box on Danforth and Main.

They hurried back in time to see a young policewoman pick up Michaela and carry her to the patrol car. The whole operation had taken less than fifteen minutes.

By their own request, Ladislav and Dora were released from their position of go-betweens in the adoption business. There were always others willing to take their place and Dora reasoned that they had made quite a bit of money, almost enough for a down payment. Houses were cheap in her western Ontario hometown. Ladislav could even buy the piece of land he had always wanted and she could have a baby of her own. Ladislav looked into his wife's eyes and saw the future for which he had come to Canada. They left Toronto for Wingham within the month. No questions asked.

Czechoslovakian Independence, 1989

Not a whole lot of people in Wingham were affected by this event.
Ladislav certainly noticed it and shed a few tears of pride and regret. But he was happy enough now. He and Dora had built their own bungalow on an acre a few miles outside of town. They had only just moved in with their own lovely baby daughter, and life was shaping up nicely. There was only one very small hiccup, a nasty reminder, when during the unpacking of boxes still sealed from their Toronto days, Dora found the birth certificate of little Michaela Velkovskova. It had been hidden in Milan Kundera's novel, *The Unbearable Lightness of Being*. This novel had been given to Ladislav as a gift by an enthusiastic Canadian aquaintance, who had been moved by the book's splendid grasp of the human predicament especially in relation to the Czech people. Written originally in French by an exiled Kundera, and translated into all the major languages of which Czech was not one, Ladya had found neither the time nor the inclination to read such profound philosophy and indeed had not mastered such eloquent prose in his new language. He had only deemed it a suitable hiding place for the birth certificate because of its Czech connection. Regarding the birth certificate, Ladya asked Dora to destroy it. It was no longer of use to Michaela Velkovskova.
On Saturday morning while Ladislav was at work, Dora tucked her sleeping baby daughter into the buggy and dropped in for a chat with

Mrs. Halley at the Old St Helens Store. Like herself, Sylvia Halley was a newcomer, set apart by circumstances from the dyed-in-the-wool attitude of some of the old-country Ontarians. While Dora had returned home with a "foreigner", Sylvia was "foreign" *and* educated. She was from England and removed enough from the locals to have earned a certain respect and admiration in Dora's eyes. Also, she made a decent cup of coffee for 75 cents and if she wasn't too busy it passed a pleasant half hour of the day. She could talk to Sylvia about Ladya's country's freedom and also share without fear or consequence her concern about the birth certificate. She approached the old general store and pushed the door open, pulling the buggy and its sleeping occupant carefully inside. "Morning, Sylvia. How's it going then?"

"Wonderfully, thank you Dora." She prepared a mug of coffee as she spoke and her nine-year-old son Robert carried it carefully over.

"Good morning Mrs.—er." Robert faltered.

"Andrasky," Dora smiled. "But you can call me Dora."

"O.K. But I like the sound when Ladya says it," Robert offered shyly.

Sylvia didn't mind a chat and it was often quiet at the Old General Store this early in the day.

"How is Alena?" she asked softly, bending over to peer at the baby, Robert at her side. "She is very pretty."

"She's doing really well, thank you. She will be one year old in a couple of weeks." acknowledged the beaming mother.

"I expect Ladya was pleased with today's news?" Sylvia continued, smiling. "It was wonderful to watch the huge peace rally in Wenceslas Square on TV last night. I wonder if that was *our* Good King Wenceslas from the Christmas carol?"

"It was. Ladya told me about him. He was their King and a Saint. I'm hoping we can visit Czechoslovakia now that it's free. Ladya says it is the most beautiful country in the world." Robert's gaze dreamily followed Dora's out of the big storefront window. She fingered the document in her pocket and made a decision.

"I need some advice," she blurted. "It's about something that happened in Toronto." Dora's eyes were filled with concern and a little fear.

Robert froze carefully. He didn't want to be sent away while the grown-ups shared critical information, and so far it seemed he had been forgotten.

"Whatever is it?" Sylvia came forward and sat down at the table to listen to Dora.

"Well, when we were in Toronto, there used to be quite a few refugees. You know? From communist countries."

"Yes? Yes?"

"There were sometimes children and babies. They needed new parents. It was terrible. Ladya and me sometimes helped. You know?'

"Yes?"

"It was only for a bit." Dora was beginning to fear she had gone too far.

"Please go on, Dora. It must have been very distressing."

"Oh yes. There was this one little girl who cried all the time and wouldn't eat." Dora began to sniffle. Robert almost fell forward he was so tense and enthralled. Sylvia hoped against hope that Dora was not going to confess to something dreadful, and suddenly remembered her son's presence.

"Robert!" she spoke sharply. He froze again.

"Oh, it's all right, Sylvia." Dora assured her. "The little girl is quite safe. I saw to that." She pulled the birth certificate from her pocket.

"It's just that I have her birth certificate here and I don't know what to do with it."

Sylvia relaxed and Robert crept forward to peer over his mother's shoulder. Dora spread the yellowed piece of paper on the table between them.

"Michaela," read Dora, "Born to Zdenek Velkovsky and Katerina Velkovskova. In the district or town," (Dora faltered over the meanings), "of Decin. On the seventh of some month in 1983." They sat back a little and Robert eased into the circle of his mother's arm.

"Why can't you send it back to her?" he asked.

"Because I don't know where she is. She was adopted by a Canadian family, and she would have been given a Canadian name by now." Robert looked at Dora in dismay and cried,

"But her real name is Michaela. Why didn't they know that?" Robert was angry. His mother gave him a warning squeeze.

"Robert! Stop it! Dora is trying to explain, and you should not even be listening to this." She turned to Dora. "Oh dear Dora, I'm sorry! Robert doesn't understand. I shouldn't have let him stay. I wasn't thinking."

"No, that's O.K. Don't worry Robert. I'll tell you what happened." And Dora prepared to embroider the truth. "We were looking after this little girl when we lived in Toronto. It was too dangerous for her to stay in her own country, you see? She was going to be adopted by Canadian parents and we were waiting for them to arrive from Alberta. But little

Michaela got very sick and we had to take her to hospital. So her new parents were going to pick her up from there, you see?" She repeated, peering at Robert sympathetically, as she wove a softer version of how she and Ladya had dumped Michaela in the park.

"I only just found the birth certificate last week when I was unpacking some boxes of books from Toronto three years ago." Dora laughed. "It's amazing how long it takes to get things done."

Robert stared at her. He sensed she was storytelling in the way some adults do for the benefit of children. He looked at his Mum. She looked puzzled.

"Dora. Didn't they need some documents at the hospital?"

"They would've prepared a report. A social service report. You know what I mean?" Dora gave Sylvia a pleading look. Sylvia thought she knew exactly what Dora meant.

"Robert! Will you please go and get some sausages from the kitchen freezer."

"But Mom . . ."

"Go!" He went, planning to be as quick as possible and Sylvia stared enquiringly at Dora.

"What really happened, Dora?"

Dora was terrified.

"I can't . . . I'm not allowed . . ." Tears brimmed in her eyes. Sylvia placed a reassuring hand over the hand across the table.

"I don't want to get you into trouble, Dora. I just want to be reassured that this child was all right. Tell me the truth."

"But Ladya . . ."

"I know, I know. Please believe this will be between you and me."

Dora took a deep breath.

"Ladya and I took her to a kids' playground near where we lived and left her there while we went to a phone box on the Danforth and called the police. We came back and watched them pick her up, so we knew she was in safe hands. Then I told Ladya we had to stop. The kids we took were smuggled in from Czechoslovakia. They were usually orphans. Michaela was our eighth, but it went wrong."

"What went wrong?"

"Michaela's own father brought her over. I understood that he was in some kind of resistance movement over there. I think his wife had been killed. Anyway, he wanted the child safely adopted in case he never got back. You could see he was afraid for his own life and his daughter's.

But Michaela was old enough to object when he tried to leave. She was so upset. And then she refused to eat or talk. I tried as best I could with her. In the end I was afraid she'd die. Sometimes you feel that no one can help these people." Tears threatened again.

"Why did you tell this to me? How did you think I could help?"

"Ladya said I was to destroy the birth certificate. It's of no use now. But somehow . . . I needed another opinion; another woman's advice. I felt that to destroy this would be like destroying Michaela's true identity for ever. Robert was right."

"*Yes!*" Hissed Robert excitedly from behind the door, clutching a frozen package of sausages. He had listened avidly to Dora's confession.

The long and the short of it was, they decided to mail the birth certificate to the Children's' Aid Department on Bloor Street in Toronto. Sylvia would do it on her visit to Toronto the following week. It would arrive as anonymously as its little owner had arrived three years previously, and with any luck or intelligence, would eventually meet up with its rightful owner.

But none of this occurred before young Robert had secretly copied her name, age and place of birth for his own reference and hidden it carefully between the pages of his favourite book of the moment; C.S. Lewis' *The Lion, the Witch and the Wardrobe*.

Part I

Guelph, Ontario 2008

Dawn was breaking on a cool October morning as Anthea marched briskly down the hill, pulling a wheeled suitcase behind her. She walked with a slight hunch, continuously prepared for attack, and yet she had a friendly demeanour. Her few friends, mostly women, found her reserved and a bit of a loner. She was on her way to the Guelph Farmers' Market. Her suitcase carried a hundred beautiful shawls to sell, all made from fine Kashmir wool, some blended with silk. Her brother had sent them from Afghanistan.

Anthea rounded the corner on the main street and found herself out of the wind. That felt better! Her wavy brown hair stopped whipping her in the face and settled calmly on her shoulders once more. It was going to be another beautiful day with a clear blue sky and trees still glowing with the unbeatable colours of an Ontario Fall. Indian summer could hardly last much longer. She turned and quickened her pace past the old town hall. The market opened at seven o'clock for the regulars and she would have to wait and see if there was a spare market table. She wanted to be inside the building as the weather grew seasonably colder, but so did the farmers and they had priority. It was now approaching eight, the magic hour when nomads such as Anthea were permitted to claim any table not yet occupied.

Suddenly there was a scream, very close, echoing icily through her blood, followed by a long drawn out howl. She spun in her tracks. A man, in well-cut jeans and a respectable looking shirt and jacket stood legs apart with eyes and arms raised to the heavens, the howl barely ended from his lips. A young woman rolled on the ground in front of him, clearly about to give vent to another scream.

Anthea added a piercing scream of her own.

"Help!" cried the girl. "He's going to hit me again." Anthea was now terrified. There was no one in sight. The town streets were deserted at this time on a Saturday morning, with the early birds at the market. There was only one thing for it and Anthea knew she had to do it.

Never, in all her thirty-five years, had she actually experienced the sensation of fighting for her life; the rush of adrenalin; the need to kill, as it were, or be killed. With a battle cry, she rushed forward and took the man in a firm jiu-jitsu hold that came intuitively to her aid from past training. She lifted and threw him in one fell swoop. There was a terrific silence for a second after he landed. Then,

"Wow!" the girl on the ground exclaimed with admiration. But,

"You stupid bitch!" yelled the man, holding his shoulder and regarding Anthea with an expression of deep pain on his face. "What the hell did you do that for?" Anthea was quite speechless. The insult she understood, but her reason for hurling him to the ground should have been abundantly clear.

The girl on the ground choked back an unruly fit of laughter behind tightly compressed lips. She rose unsteadily to her feet and went over to the fuming man on the sidewalk, now sitting upright but still protectively holding his shoulder. She reached out her hand, offering to help him to his feet. He growled and accepted.

"Poor Ian!" she whispered, her voice cooing.

"Shut up, you idiot! Why on earth did you say I was going to hit you?"

"I just couldn't resist." She turned towards Anthea. "I'm so sorry. I became extremely faint and dizzy and I fell over. If I had been holding on to Ian as he had asked, I wouldn't have fallen. I couldn't help screaming. It startled me." Her face took on a rueful expression. Anthea glanced at Ian, rising grimly to his feet, and asked,

"Do you mean you just called out to tease him, to make me think you were being attacked?"

"'Fraid so!" The rueful expression deepened as Ian marched off without a word.

"I've done it now," she said unconcernedly. "Would you mind walking with me as far as the market? Just in case it happens again."

"Oh, certainly. Of course. Shall I take your arm?"

"Thanks. My name's Ofelia, with an f. What's yours?"

"Anthea," she said briefly. The time was getting on and Anthea was beginning to worry she might have forfeited her place at the market. She could see this little event costing her a couple of hundred dollars and she was annoyed at the thoroughly casual attitude of this person.

"Don't be cross," Ofelia offered with a fine sense of timing. "It's not quite eight yet and I know for a fact that there will be a space for you. Ian and I were off to market as well. We were taking over from a friend who couldn't be there. You can have her place, because you see now we won't be there either." She cast a dazzling smile at Anthea who stared back, not sure whether to become even more exasperated or not.

If she could have seen into the future, she would have known that such experiences were the norm when you played a part in the life of Ofelia with an f. For now, she satisfied herself by cocking her head questioningly, not trusting herself to speak.

Ofelia was a lively girl. Slight of build with dancing eyes set in a fine-featured face, her unruly dark hair gave her an exotic, almost Romany look that was emphasized by her flowing skirt and colourful jewellery. Excitement was surging through her as she walked down the street, arm in arm with this complete stranger. It was the kind of excitement that hit you when something extraordinary was about to happen.

This time a door will open, Ofelia thought fervently. *I know it will*. She had known it the moment the faintness had overcome her. *It was a sign*. She skipped lightly, causing the woman beside her to cast her a forbidding glance. Ofelia sent back a disarming smile. She could understand the discomfiture she must be causing.

As a small child, she had been secure and well loved, but she had been adopted and could not quite relinquish a sense of loss and therefore hope, that still tugged at her. She could never forget the desolation and pain of being torn away from a life she could no longer clearly remember. She had been unable to communicate. The sounds that emerged from the mouths of the people of her new environment made no sense to her ears, so she did not speak. The man and the woman and the three older boys with whom she had been finally placed in Guelph, had cared for her kindly. They had hugged her unresponsive body and smothered her with love and laughter until gradually, very gradually, a transformation had taken place and she had softened and the sounds of their mouths began to make sense. The words became language and any other language she had once spoken in another world, was buried. She began to talk again.

Her own sweetness of nature crept back into her being and soon her loneliness was assuaged by loving parents and three brothers. But her never-ending secret purpose in life was to solve the mystery of her birthright.

Anthea walking beside her, was not to know the chain of events about to be set in motion.

At the Market

When they reached the market, Ofelia took off her coat and helped Anthea set up her shawls on the table. While chatting in a friendly fashion, Anthea noticed that Ofelia wore a beautiful old shawl of her own. She remarked upon it. Ofelia said that she believed it was from somewhere in Eastern Europe, whereupon Anthea shared that her mother had spent some time teaching in the Czech Republic the previous year. Ofelia promptly asked if she could meet Anthea's mother.

Anthea was taken aback. She was reluctant to send such an unpredictable stranger to her mother's address. On the other hand, her mother had no such qualms and would perhaps welcome the distraction. After brief consideration, Anthea decided she *would* send Ofelia off to her mother's address on King Street and having done so, she focused her attention on the business of the market.

Here, she was in her element. Her shawls were displayed all around her now, some hanging from a small stand. They were exotic, colourful and very popular. People stopped to admire and try them on. Old ladies, loving the fabric's texture, bought them to drape over sofas or as early Christmas gifts for daughters and granddaughters. Men bought them for wives and girlfriends. More women turned them over on the table and bought two or three at a time. Anthea always gave them a deal when they bought more than two. She agreed with these women; you could not have too many shawls or scarves. You could double them and loop them round your neck, simply tie them singly, use them as a wrap over whatever you were wearing for extra warmth or you could even make a mini skirt out of them if you wished. "Like a sarong," begged a young teenager, turning to her mom for the appropriate amount of cash.

"Excuse me," a voice murmured. Anthea looked around and was surprised to see Ian standing sheepishly beside her.

"Oh! Ian!" Anthea said. "How are you? I hope you're all right after my throwing you down like that. I was pretty scared at the time."

"It's okay." Ian brushed this aside. "Where's Ofelia gone?"

"Actually, she went to see my mother." Ian's sheepish demeanor disappeared in a flash.

"Good God! Why? Does she know her?"

"No, probably not. But we were talking and I noticed her shawl. She said she had owned it all her life, that it was a connection with her past life . . ."

"Did she tell you anything else?" interrupted Ian.

"Like what?"

"Like anything at all!" he snapped.

"No!" Anthea snapped back. This guy with his rather snobbish British accent was beginning to annoy her. She decided all at once that she was not going to tell him anything more than she had to.

"Ofelia said she'd probably return to the market or else go on home, if that helps." She turned to a new customer, ignoring Ian's presence.

Ian walked off with bad grace and no word of farewell. Anthea allowed her thoughts to wander in her mother's direction. How had her mother received Ofelia and had Ofelia and she got on and talked about the shawl's pattern? *I'll bet they're having a cup of tea right now*, she thought, and smiled. Her mother had altogether too much imagination and still retained a childlike desire for adventure. Sometimes Anthea wished her mother would act like other mothers or women of her age, and be "normal", whatever normal meant. Her whole family was a bit strange. She liked it for the most part; it added spice to life.

Take the market for example. That had an element of intrigue and was full of interesting people. It teemed with life. The earliest shoppers sought produce and staples and carried their shopping home for breakfast and an early start to the weekend. Others came later, to browse and enjoy the atmosphere. These were all regular participants of Guelph's market life and they came out of habit, bringing guests and friends and meeting others for organic coffee and chats.

One such partaker was George Hojack. George was a tall man of fifty-some years, slightly overweight with fading blond hair and light blue eyes. He had a pleasant outgoing character and a genuine liking for people. He was therefore often well liked in return, but he had an inclination to linger. He had arrived on the dot of eight and felt quite virtuous about it. His daughter Carly was with him, sent by Mum to keep him on track. They were getting supplies from Cleo who ran Stark Naked Naturals, a company which sold beautiful lotions and creams, completely natural and deliciously flavoured with essential oils.

Stark Naked Naturals, commonly known as Starkers, was trading busily as George and Carly arrived. Cleo saw them out of the corner of her eye as she expounded upon the efficacy of her calendula body butter to an awe-inspired customer. *Good Lord!* thought Cleo. *What am I going to do now?* George loved to chat and thought the market was the place to do it. He especially liked to talk to her but as far as she could tell, he had no concept of business, and she did not have time. George viewed the market as a social gathering, which of course it was, depending on your point of view and how dependent you were on your business. Cleo did not come here to play. She came to earn money. Luckily, George bumped into a crony and they sauntered off towards the coffee stand. Cleo noticed the crestfallen expression on Carly's face and sympathised. She finished counting out the change to her customer, who had bought three pots of butter, making Cleo feel generous.

"Hey Carly! Come and give us a hand. It's busy here."

Cleo was a chocolate brown island girl, tall and willowy with short curling hair and delicate tendrils lying tenderly on her long neck. To look at her, you'd think butter wouldn't melt in her mouth. But she was a business woman of such high calibre that not only did she earn financial independence at the market on a Saturday morning, but spent the week managing a small team of workers who saw to it that the products of Stark Naked Naturals were shipped worldwide. She was a veritable slave driver, milking her staff just short of dry and rewarding them for their hard work with charm and generosity and occasional cash bonuses.

But here was Carly and she needed her. They needed each other.

"Hi Cleo!" Carly smiled her relief and slipped behind the market table. She liked playing shop. She was good at it and Cleo always treated her seriously.

"Thanks, Sweetie. Now you go round to the front and straighten out those jars for me. The moment another customer appears you whip round here again and we'll serve them together." Carly enjoyed the teamwork. Together they would pack, gift wrap and mark off sales.

Carly would even accept money from customers and hand back change. And if her Dad didn't come back too soon, Cleo would likely give her five bucks for helping.

George, in fact, had settled at a table with a large mug of coffee and his old friend Jimmy. Jimmy was a person who thrived on stories of his opulent past. George, who had grown up with Jimmy on Snob Hill, knew all these stories off by heart and knew well how to head Jimmy off onto other subjects. George had an important subject of his own to discuss. He was threatened and devastated by his own news item, and Jimmy, a veritable old woman for gossip, would love it. Jimmy had always shown a typical bachelor's intolerance for George's wife Ann, and this morning, Ann had threatened to leave with all three kids if he, George, could not pull his weight in the family.

George had an amiable and loving personality, well off financially because his mother had left enough to discourage his incentive to work. He'd had plenty of handouts during her lifetime as well. But she had sadly failed in handing down her own work ethic. The lovely old brick house, in which he lived with his wife and three children, was mortgage-free with two good cars parked in the driveway in a very desirable part of town and within reach of all the amenities. Life, on the whole, was good!

But Jim was launching into the latest episode from the saga of how he had been cheated of his inheritance, which George had heard the week before. George had to intercept.

"I know, I know, Jim. Don't bullshit me with that stuff. Get up off your backside and get proactive for once in your life."

"Ha! You're a fine one to talk," Jim said. "Get proactive yourself. Get a job." With difficulty, George refrained from resorting to four letter words and said,

"Listen Buddy, I'm in trouble." Jimmy was immediately all ears.

"Shoot Buddy. I'm listening."

"Ann's getting worried. She thinks I'm not pulling my weight."

Jimmy made a choking noise. A lady from the next table left hurriedly.

"This is serious. She's going to leave me."

"Good! About time."

"What do you mean by that?"

"I mean that it's about time you stopped hiding behind a skirt and came and got on with your life."

"You've never liked her, have you?" George said. "You've never been able to see her worth, have you? You yourself can't get a woman to stay with you any length of time so you demonstrate your jealousy by denigrating Ann."

Jimmy's laughter pealed across the market, causing two more people to rise and leave.

"You are such an unbelievable asshole . . ." Without warning an arm descended heavily on George's shoulder.

"Excuse me sir, but would you and your friend please continue your conversation away from the vicinity of the market?" A security officer smiled very firmly at them. She was Lois, and she was both big and strong, an ex-mud wrestler in her day and a very ex-girlfriend of Jimmy's.

"Good morning Lois!" Jimmy was all charm. "We were just leaving anyway. And how's Buster doing?" he asked, referring to Lois' Japanese wrestling dog that had once pinned him mercilessly on the floor at her command when he had refused to leave her apartment. She had threatened to break his fingers. Two hundred pounds of dog had allowed him to rise after his promise to obey and he had left with as much dignity as possible. And that *was* some, being Jimmy.

Outside, Jimmy turned up Gordon Street.

"Come with me. I'm in an apartment just next to Harvey's. You want to see it?"

"An apartment? You mean where you pay *rent*?" George was surprised. Jimmy was invariably "staying" with someone.

"Of course not, you idiot. Remember Mike the Pike? He had to make himself scarce for a few weeks so he asked me to do him a favour and care-take for him while he was away."

George shook his head in disbelief. And then remembered his daughter.

"Gotta go. I left Carly in the market."

"Huh! No wonder you're in trouble all the time. Good luck. I'm sure the problem with Ann's not serious," and with a chuckle Jimmy was gone. George shook his head and stared after him, his heart sinking as he thought of his wife's ultimatum. In twenty years of marriage it had never come to this. He needed to talk to someone. Cleo would be good; she was sympathetic and extremely practical. He suspected that she rather fancied him but she could be standoffish if she felt like it so he would have to tread carefully. He could see that Carly was having fun helping so he did not hurry. He stopped in at Nora's Armenian vegetarian stand

and bought half a dozen dolma. He made his way towards Stark Naked Naturals, armed, as he thought, with gifts of food. Cleo saw him.

"Hello George. Remembered Carly did you? Well you can leave her with me. We are doing O.K."

"Yes Dad. Can I stay?" Carly noticed the stuffed vine leaves in his hand. "Ugh Dad! What's that?" Cleo leaned over to examine.

"Mmm. Dolma. O.K. if you like that sort of thing. Too early for me. George! Would you be a dear and fetch me a coffee and one of those ham and fried egg toasted English muffins? Here's some money. Do you want one too, Carly?"

"Oo yeah. I love them. No coffee though. Thank you, Cleo." Carly grinned.

George, snubbed, turned without taking the money. He returned with their order after a ten-minute line up and passed it over to the outstretched hands of a busy and distracted Cleo. Disconsolately, he continued through the market until he espied Anthea. She appeared to be dreaming on her feet.

"Wake up! Anthea!" George was at her side with an offering of food. She turned with a start and saw the plateful of stuffed vine leaves.

"Oo-oo! Lovely. Thanks George. You arrived at exactly the right moment. Mmm. My favourite!" Anthea gobbled up a dolma with relish and George positively glowed.

"How are you? And how is that lovely mother of yours?"

"Oh, Mom, she's fine. I think she might be in her element right now. I sent her a mysterious visitor." George looked interested. Anthea privately thought George had a crush on her mother.

"I met this girl called Ofelia on the way to market this morning. I happened to knock her boyfriend down because I thought he was hitting her. But he wasn't. Anyway, *he* stomped off and Ofelia came along with me to the market. I noticed she was wearing a lovely old shawl. She said it was a shawl she had had since before she was adopted at the age of about three. She didn't know anything else about it, just that it was her only connection with her past."

"Interesting," said George, in a voice that showed he wanted to hear more.

"Well, you know Mom. The pattern on the shawl looked sort of Middle European." Anthea grinned. "Mom's been acting bored again lately. I thought that Ofelia and her shawl might give her something to take an interest in."

"Gosh! Yes!" George's eyes searched for a horizon. "I'll bet I could be of help there. I think I'll drop round and see her. But tell me more about knocking this guy over. I didn't think of you as violent, Anthea."

"I'm not violent. I just mistook the situation, that's all. I'll tell you about it another time. I'm busy now."

"Okay, fine," George smiled. "I'll hold you to that." And he left, leaving the plate of remaining dolma behind. Anthea was not sure whether to be pleased about him visiting her mother or not, but whatever happened, her mother could handle it.

A few moments later she saw Carly go by with a friend. She *had* meant to ask after Ann and the kids.

A Plan Evolves

Edda did her best thinking over the kitchen sink. She was a smaller version of her daughter with beautiful auburn hair, compliments of today's up to the minute hair salon care. There was a perpetual air of restlessness and purpose about her. She had boundless energy with nowhere to go, as if it were caged and prowling; almost dangerous. She thought of her son in Kandahar. As a mother she had long ago ceased to fear for him, and as an extension of self she was proud of him; glad that he had had the courage to brave an unknown and untried frontier.

The fact was Bruno was a bit of a rake. A couple of scandals invented by no less than three girlfriends had quite fairly evened the score and sent him running to the comparative peace of Kandahar, where his intrepid and somewhat sergeant-majorish personality found favour and solace among the flying shells and clear-cut pecking order. Nonetheless Edda wished he would stop renewing his contract with them.

But he likes living on the edge, she thought. *Thank God he was not actually in the military or he would never come home. He could never have known before he went what it would be really like to live there.*

It is only within our imagination that we know how it would be to live in a war zone. Bruno himself had said that his greatest culture shock was returning to Canada; to the quiet complacency of home.

How Edda wished to escape from the quiet complacency of home. Her thoughts took wings and flew over Afghanistan, over dusty mountain ranges and sprawling forest where groups of bandit Taliban lay in wait.

Spiralling down, she saw scorched sandstone towns with crowded market places and narrow streets. Heavily shrouded women hurried swiftly and secretly along in the shadows. There lay the camp near Kandahar city, as big as a town, and she could see the rockets crashing into it out of the clear blue sky; fiery mushrooms of cloud rising into the air and tiny figures rushing madly in all directions beneath. Others rushed towards the crash site to help the wounded. Oh no! More rockets coming! Edda sighed and gave up. She would never picture it accurately. All she knew was that *she* did not want to be there among that sad devastation. However, she did want to be somewhere else, desperately. Anywhere but here. Round in circles went the thoughts:

What was wrong with "here"?

That she had hit her sixtieth birthday might have had something to do with the desperation. The "end" was in sight and there was so much remaining to be done that had been put off. It was true that marriage and children took up a good few years, but what had happened to the time after the children had left home, married and with kids of their own? She had been a widow for over ten years now and what had she done of note in that time?

Nothing!

Oh, but she had a home and a part-time job working for a friend who owned a natural body care company. Why was this not enough?

Was it because of India? She had always wanted to travel to India. Edda sighed out loud. She gazed unseeing out of her kitchen window. From nowhere, a wind had sprung to chase the leaves from the late maple on the lawn. A sharp rapping on her front door brought Edda back from her reveries. She dried her hands, went to the door and found herself looking into the friendly smiling face of a young woman in her early twenties; a face framed by unruly curls that did not look as if they had been brushed that morning. Edda was compelled to see beyond to the sparkling personality beneath.

"Hello! Edda? My name's Ofelia. Anthea sent me." A sense of unreality descended upon Edda. *Edda; Ofelia; Anthea.* How strange! How theatrical! She continued to stare at the girl.

"Can I come in?"

"Well, yes." Edda thought she must sound rude but could not shake off her dreamlike state.

"I have something to show you," Ofelia appealed, as if she suspected her own lack of substance.

"Please do come in." Edda drew back to allow her entrance. "I was struck by our names," she explained, leading the way into the living room.

"Really? Why is that?"

"Edda, Ofelia and Anthea. Three names not often heard and perhaps never before heard together."

"Oh," Ofelia said offhandedly. "I feel very much at ease among unusual names. Take Ofelia, for instance." She had left her shoes in the hallway and was now perched on the sofa, her legs curled beneath her. "My name was Mary Morton until I was five. Mary Morton! Can you believe it?"

"Well, what's the matter with it?" Edda asked in surprise.

"Did your mother name you Edda? Are you in fact English? I mean actually from England? I mean Edda is more of a Scandinavian name I think."

Edda smiled and admitted that she had in fact been christened Edna Joy.

"Joy is nice."

"But Edna! I absolutely hated the name Edna when I was young. I made people call me Ed, which wasn't much better I suppose. Would you like a cup of coffee?"

"I'd prefer herbal tea please, if you have any. I'll come with you." They made their way into the kitchen while Edda continued to speak, saying that she had changed her name when she moved from the provinces to London about forty years ago in England. And yes, she *had* known it was a Swedish name and she had liked it. Still did. Ofelia asked her how old she had been when that happened.

"Twenty."

"I was fourteen when I changed mine. We were doing *Hamlet* in school and I was much taken with Ophelia's story. I also thought that the surname, Morton, which I had been given on the papers I arrived in Guelph with, had a ring of death that went well with Ophelia. I spelled it with an "f" to be different. I had been Mary Kingsley after I was officially adopted of course, but I reverted to 'Morton' for a while when I was fourteen. Hormones, I suppose. The 'Morton' part never stuck, one way and another."

Edda was slightly taken aback, but had to admit the girl was unusual and therefore probably warranted unusual behaviour.

"I was abandoned when I was three," Ofelia went on. "Someone found me in a park in Toronto. It took another two years before I was properly adopted. My foster family here in Guelph decided to keep me." Edda's heart contracted at Ofelia's cool, matter of fact delivery.

"You were found in a park?"

"Yes, I was." Ofelia scrabbled among the various tisanes kept by her hostess. She found something called "Mmm! Tea" and chose that one.

"What's this?"

"Melissa, Marigold and Mint. Lovely with a bit of honey. Shall I make you a cup?"

"Please." They soon settled with their hot drinks with the question of Ofelia's abandonment hanging in the air. There was hesitation on both sides. Edda waited, preparing to change the subject to something less sensitive.

"I've never told anyone this before," Ofelia now said, slanting a shy look in Edda's direction. "I was afraid people would think I was being my usual fanciful self."

She began to tell her story.

"My very first memory of my life was a sudden huge red glow in the night. It was all over the place; as if there had been an explosion. I don't remember a bang, though, because everything was silent, absolutely silent. The air was full of swirling objects; flying debris I suppose. I was cold because we were outside. I was wrapped, but I remember the frosty air. Someone held me in his arms. It was my father. I *know* it was my father." Edda stared in fascination. Ofelia continued, "We were running far away from the explosion. I remember reaching some kind of dwelling and being taken in and given warm milk. I remember the warm milk because it tasted horrible, but I drank it. I hate warm milk. People were talking all around me but I couldn't hear a thing. They put me to bed and the next morning a rooster was crowing outside and I jumped up to see it. I could obviously hear again. We were on some kind of farm. It was a scruffy kind of place and I didn't know where I was. I was frightened and wanted my father. This was not Canada and I was not speaking English."

"Oh my goodness!" Edda was round-eyed, a good audience. Ofelia glanced at Edda. "After this, it is hard to remember the exact course of events. We travelled a lot, staying in different places, always on the move. Eventually, we got on an airplane, which took us to a new land. I remember I couldn't understand what people were saying and that I was terribly distressed. I used to cry and have tantrums over nothing." Edda's hand itched to reach out to Ofelia's as she picked at the threads on her loose Indian top.

"The last words my father said to me as he went away were that we would be together again. I understood it in the old language, but somehow I can't say the words any more, except for the last one, which was I think a term of endearment. I'm not sure. Ofelia's distress was palpable.

Myshka's father's last words to his daughter had been:

"We will be together again Myshka my darling"

Myshko milachku.

The words were imprinted in her heart. She would not speak them but she would see him again.

"What were the words?" demanded Edda, but Ofelia only shook her head vehemently and could not speak for a moment.

"We were in Canada," Ofelia continued. "I remember a small and rather grubby apartment and a young couple. The woman used to try and encourage me to eat but I threw up. I don't know why. She was quite kind to me. I remember her saying, 'Come on darling! Eat up.' I must have got really sick because the next thing I remember was being in a big hospital in a big, big bed with doctors examining me and nurses trying to make me take medication and food. I fought them off every step of the way. I suppose they must have tranquilised me; maybe put me on a drip for food and medication because I got better. I was eventually taken away by the authorities and put in a foster home. Apparently I battled these foster people too. I wouldn't eat or speak. I just screamed whenever they tried to feed me or make me do anything. The authorities estimated me to be about three years old and had named me after the street nearest to where I had been found in the park; Morton Street. Soon after that, a foster family from Guelph agreed to take me. They eventually adopted me and by dint of pure persistence and love, they won me over. I began to trust them and, yes, even to love them. And so, I thrived at last." Here, Ofelia cast an intense look at Edda, whose eyes were glistening.

"But I never forgot my father, and I never discovered what happened to him. One day I'm going to find out. I know I am. I have never actually told my story to anyone before. Not so completely, anyway. Not even my boyfriend Ian."

"Why are you telling me then?"

"Because I feel that somehow you are going to help me."

"And when," Edda asked, "did you reach that conclusion?"

"While I was standing on your doorstep waiting to be asked in."

"You asked yourself in."

"I know, but it wasn't because you didn't want me to come in, was it? It was because you were taken with all our names. I knew then that you were going to have special meaning in my life." There was silence while they both sank into their own thoughts.

Edda recognised that her life had swung into an entirely new direction. She felt as though deliverance had come to her in the person of this young woman. But she could not fathom what form it would take. Whatever did it all mean? Ofelia was holding something out and speaking.

"Sorry! What did you say?"

"I said that Anthea asked me to show you this."

Ofelia spread out her shawl to display the pattern. You could see that it was old, but the faded beautiful colours clearly indicated the woven symbol of a right hand holding a scythe with the initials NJ underneath.

"I was wearing this when they found me in Toronto. They let me keep it because I was so obviously attached to it." Slowly, Edda leaned forward and gently took the shawl from Ofelia. She held it up in complete disbelief at the symbol as the room began to slowly spin and she thought she would faint.

The market eventually drew to a close. It was twelve o'clock. Anthea packed away the remaining shawls, and bought some cheese from the sheep lady at Shepherd's Purse, and sunflower sprouts from Mireille from Montreal and was soon headed out. On the way she hailed Cleo, who asked after her mother. Cleo and her mother went back a long way. Anthea retraced her steps through the town centre and was home in fifteen minutes.

She rented the small upstairs apartment at her mother's house on King Street, which was convenient as they both travelled a lot, though rarely together and rarely at the same time. She had her own front door right next to her mother's. They shared the porch and as Anthea turned the key in her own lock, she could hear activity in her mother's hallway. Someone was leaving. Not wishing to encroach, she let herself in quickly and closed her door. Seconds later, through the glass, she observed her mother letting out both George and Ofelia and waving them an enthusiastic goodbye. Edda caught sight of Anthea peeking through the glass and excitedly beckoned her in. Anthea came with alacrity, dying to know what had transpired.

"Oh Anthea!" Edda was all aglow. "You will *never* believe this!"

"I probably will."

"Ofelia's shawl. You are so clever, darling. That pattern on the shawl, how did you know?"

"I didn't actually *know*. I just guessed it might mean something to you. It looked kind of familiar. Did you recognise it or something?"

"Yes! Yes! Absolutely!" Edda was beside herself. "This must seem impossible, I know, but that was the emblem of the town in the Czech Republic where I taught last year. I nearly fainted. I had to go and check. In the end I went online and pulled up the site for the city of Novy Jicin and there it was, as clear as can be: the shoulder and right arm of a medieval man holding a scythe. I couldn't believe it. Ofelia sat down and had a good cry."

"Do . . . do you mean that . . . that there's a connection between . . ." Anthea stuttered.

"I mean that Ofelia seems to have come from Novy Jicin."

"Didn't she know where she came from?" Anthea asked, aghast.

"Not really, but that's another story which I'm sure she'll tell you soon. Meanwhile, there is a lot to be done." Edda became practical.

"And what about George?"

"Well, George came in at the end of the discussion and we didn't tell him much; just that we had traced the symbol on Ofelia's shawl. He originates from Slovakia, you know, so from an old Czechoslovakian point of view, he took quite a personal interest."

"But what are you going to do? What can you do?" Anthea's brain was not working at the same pace as her mother's.

"We can go to Novy Jicin and track her family down."

"But . . ." Anthea did not know where to begin. "Mom!" she wailed. "Think first."

Edda looked at her daughter in surprise.

"I have thought," she retorted. "And this seems the clearest way. You'll see. Wait until I explain. George says he wants to come too, though I think he's dreaming. He still has a bit of the language that he learned from his mother. Anyway that's neither here nor there, really. He was just on the look-out for an adventure and wants to be included." Edda dismissed the idea with a wave of the hand.

The Ofelia Project

Ofelia wandered thoughtfully downtown to catch a bus home. She wondered if Ian would be there or not. She hoped he wouldn't. He was too demanding and she wanted to be on her own to think. She hadn't told Ian the true story of her past. She had not, as she had told Edda, shared it with anyone. She was afraid she would be pitied and did not want that. She had always had a feeling that she was from an old Eastern Block country, based on the fact that when she was about five she had heard some people speaking in a foreign language and had asked her adopted mother what they were saying.

"I don't understand them, Mary. I think they are Poles." Little Mary did not understand the meaning of Poles in a geographical context until she was older, but at the time she felt that the words which were so familiar to her ear, must convict her of being some kind of a stick, and her new mother had unintentionally sounded a little off hand. Of course, Little Mary had been awfully insecure during this phase of her life and had kept it a great secret within her heart that she was descended from a pole. Even when she eventually understood that she might be of Polish origin, she had still kept it to herself. Anyway she discovered that she could not understand Polish when she heard it in later years. Thus, Mary, who became rebellious Ofelia, felt herself to be of middle-European heritage, but more than this she could not guess. All she had was the shawl.

The bus carried her to the northeast corner of town where she rented a cosy one-bedroom apartment. It followed an eclectic style of décor with Indian saris hanging gracefully from the windows and large Indian cushions and throws over her battered sofa. The walls were painted a dark parchment colour, which she had stippled to resemble old outside walls that you might find in a Mediterranean harbour town. The many paintings on her walls were her own, beautifully framed. A large orange cat stretched himself lazily at her arrival, meowed in greeting or complaint and promptly went to sleep again.

The kitchen was small and very untidy. It had a counter overlooking the dining area and every cup, dish, pot and pan was spread about. A pot of honey sat open with a buttery knife in it. A loaf of organic sprouted bread lay with its plastic bag open and the peeping slices of bread going stale fast.

"Ian was here!" She stated, giving each word equal emphasis. Pause, the cat, gave another half-hearted meow. Ofelia tightened the bread bag and put it in the fridge. She lifted the knife carefully from the honey, licked it clean, and was happy to see that not too much butter had come off in the jar, as she liked her honey for sweetening tea. Quickly she gathered the pans, which she herself had left out. She put all the dirty dishes in the sink and wiped the counter carefully. Then she went into the bedroom where her worst fears were realised. Ian lay flat out on her bed, pretending to be asleep.

"I know you're awake. What are you doing?"

"I'm having a rest waiting for you," he said, as though it should be obvious.

"Well, I want you to go home."

"What?" Ian said. "Why? Especially after the way you treated me this morning; making that woman think I was a wife abuser."

"Don't *ever* think of me as a wife. I am not and never will be your wife. Also, you don't live here and I don't like the way you come in making yourself at home, leaving me a mess to clean up. I'm not your mother either. God help your mother." Ofelia turned and went back to the living room. Ian was after her like a shot.

"What's happened? You are different. You were quite happy with me last night." He gave her a sideways look. "You know you were." Ofelia didn't respond to this line of attack.

"I'm not different. I'm moving on."

"What do you mean, 'moving on'?"

"Stop asking so many questions, Ian. I've got a lot to think about right now. When I'm ready, I'll tell you and if you keep going on at me like this I'll tell you nothing." Ofelia could be extremely focused when she wanted and nothing would deter her when she was in this mood. At this moment, Ian, whom she quite liked but with whom she had never been in love, had dropped to the bottom of her priorities. Oh yes, he was good in bed, but easily replaced, she figured. She desperately wanted to be alone to think. She went back into the bedroom (followed by Ian), picked up his jacket off the floor, opened the window to let in some fresh air, and spoke:

"Look, Ian, I'm sorry I appear to be such a bitch, but I'll call you tonight. Or why don't you call me and we'll talk. I can't think clearly right now."

"Arrrgh! It's all about *you* isn't it?" Ian fumed, snatching his coat and preparing to slam the door.

"The trouble with you is you think everyone should be at your beck and call, don't you? Well I'm not!" and the apartment resounded with the slamming echo he left.

Takes one to know one. Ofelia thought as she prepared herself a sparse lunch. She was vegan and ate like a bird, but appeared to thrive on it.

She ate on the sofa beside Pause, who purred briefly.

So, she was Czech. She felt the joy of her identity wash over her. The language she had heard as a child must have been Czech, not Polish and she would have still been able to understand it at that time. She wondered if any of the Czech language remained in her memory at all. Only two words sprang into her mind: "Myshka" she could hear as if in a dream, and the word "Milatchku!" which enveloped her in warmth. Now she would check out the Czech language. *Check Czech.*

It had begun this morning with Anthea, as she had known it would. At last the door was opening.

Edda, who had unbelievably spent a year in that very town where her history had begun, seemed almost as excited as herself. But should they both get involved? Or was this a solitary quest? She felt fearful. She wanted to share this almost unbeknownst burden she had been carrying. She wanted a partner, and Edda was a godsend. Her adoptive parents were true parents to her; they had put up with her moods and tantrums in those traumatic teenage years. And yet they had never encouraged her to look into her past. They seemed to want her to believe that she was all theirs. Would she feel like that if *she* ever adopted a child? She did not want to hurt her parents by keeping secrets, so she would go and talk to them about her discovery, of course. She owed them that. But beyond that . . . hopefully they would wish her well and support her desire to find her roots. She thought briefly about Anthea, the magical connection. She must get organised. She grabbed a notebook and wrote.

1. Give notice at work.
2. Arrange care for apartment and Pause.
3. Book flight to Prague.
4. Book into hostel/hotel.
5. Check train and bus timetables for the town of Novy Jicin.

Ofelia closed her book and stared at the ceiling. This needed a little more thought.

George crept back into his house. It was only just noon and Ann was not yet home from work. He admitted to himself that he was nervous. His wife was not an ogre by any means. She was always very kind. She had just given him enough rope to hang himself, that's all. George removed his coat and hung it up. He emptied his pockets out of habit onto the kitchen windowsill. He heard the front door open. He went to help her. He knew she would have shopping. They looked at each other expectantly. George was the first to look away as he turned to take the groceries to the kitchen. She followed him in.

"Did you get my marigold body butter from Cleo?" she asked quietly. George's heart fell to his stockinged feet.

"Er . . . I think Carly's got it." He felt like an idiot.

"Where is Carly?"

"She met Meghan in the market. She'll be back shortly I expect."

"You know that Meghan is trouble, don't you? I'm surprised she was up early enough to be in the market."

Carly can cope." George was at least confident about this.

"She shouldn't have to cope. You shouldn't have left her. Who did you meet this time? I hope not that Jimmy."

"Actually I visited Edda because she had a young person there who had some connection with Czechoslovakia, as it used to be, and I thought I could be of some help."

"And could you?" Ann was relentless and George was honest and obedient.

"I could be, as it happens. The girl has discovered she stems from the same town that Edda was teaching in a year or two ago. It's an amazing coincidence. She wants to find her roots. Apparently she was adopted without knowing about . . ."

"Stop it George. Just don't say any more."

"For goodness sakes, Ann! Hear me out."

"No. I'm afraid of what I'm going to hear. You seem to take more interest in someone else's problems than in taking care of your own family." George was crestfallen because he dearly loved his family, wife and all. He cared for them, and looked after the house and cooking and did most of the grocery shopping too. His wife went out to work; she had a well-paid position. George occasionally worked translating German magazine articles for a national journal, but was not inclined to take too many of these. He was indolent by nature. George also knew that he felt inadequate. He had no career as most other men had, and so was unable to put up an argument in his own defence. He was a kept man. Secretly, when he had heard Ofelia's story, he was ready to take off at once and launch into some exciting detective work. But then he would have had to leave his family. In addition, the job might have carried an element of danger in it.

"It's not that you don't have a job, George, it's that you don't *want* a job." Well, that took the wind out of his last thought! It was true. He did not want a job. He felt a heavy depression settle on him and sat down on the nearest kitchen chair. It gave way beneath him, (he had meant to fix it all week), and he crashed to the floor, banging his head on the corner of the stove as he went down.

He sat up groggily to find all three daughters looming anxiously over him. The oldest, Sarah, back from university for a weekend visit, pronounced him "O.K." and returned to her room. Tracy, almost eighteen, sniffed in a derogatory manner, and asked if he were drunk. George gave her a hurt look.

Carly, home again, said, "Hi Dad! Wow you've got a big bump coming on your head. Does it hurt?"

George groaned and started to his feet. Though Carly was the only one who gave him a hand, Ann had automatically reached for the peroxide and a swab to attend to the graze on his scalp. The chair was history. Several parts had snapped. As he gathered up the pieces and took them down through the basement to the garage, he wondered what the hell he was going to do with himself. To think that he had been excited about the Ofelia project. To think that he could have actually imagined becoming involved in helping this girl find her relatives. Who did he think he was? He reached up for some cord and carefully tied the pieces of chair together, ready for the garbage pickup on Tuesday, then went sadly to the kitchen to apologise once again to his long suffering wife.

But Ann had reached the end of her tether with her husband and had left the house on foot for Cleo's before George came back from the garage. In her distress, she had not noticed that Carly had in fact put her order of body butter from Stark Naked Naturals right on the kitchen table for her.

Cleo lived in a stylish bungalow a couple of streets over from the Hojak's house. Her husband, William, was a self made man. He earned a lot of money and appeared to be as cold and aloof a person as you could ever hope to meet.

Brought up in England by a domineering father and a meek and timid mother, he had removed himself from their influence at the age of fifteen by running away. He had worked odd jobs in London and received an entirely new education on the streets. By the time he was eighteen, he had returned to school to catch up on his formal education.

He got a job after that and put himself through university with the help of the state. He then became a very successful chartered accountant. He soon immigrated to Canada having landed himself a top position in a well-known Ontarian company. He eventually started his own accounting firm and had never looked back.

He must have learned enough from his father's attitude, (unless it was in his genes), to be hard and wilful in business, bidding for new accounts and proving himself the best man for the job in almost every case. He had no time for fools and considered most people to be fools. Women especially he tended to despise, and therefore was still a bachelor and already quite well off when he met his future wife while on a holiday in Trinidad. Cleo's mother owned the hotel he was staying at and he was already impressed, in spite of himself, with the way she ran the business. Then she introduced him to her lovely twenty-year-old daughter. William was astounded. He had never looked twice at a girl in England, especially not at a girl of alien culture or colour. When he had arrived in Canada he had ceased looking at the fair and foolish sex altogether. Now, he fell head over heels and completely in love with Cleo. He slipped unconsciously into the kind, carefree and happy young man that he always should have been and Cleo fell in love with this version of the man. She wooed him with her delightful island charm. Cleo had an attitude to life that knew nothing of "colour". She did not know she was "black". And so William saw it that way too.

"Come! I show you how we dance," and William discovered that moving to the sinuous calypso music opened a passageway to his starved emotions. Cleo played the piano for him and her husky voice delivered the blues into his very soul. She completely healed him.

William commuted back and forth from Toronto to Trinidad and the whirlwind romance resulted in an island wedding after only three months of courtship.

Unfortunately, when they returned to live in Canada, within a year William had reverted to his old self, which made both of them very unhappy. William watched the light leave Cleo's eyes and recognised his own mother's plight, but he was entirely unable to help it. The additional fact that no babies came along to temper their life had perhaps intensified their difficulties.

Cleo eventually rose above it all by starting her own business making soap in her kitchen as a "nice little pastime" and had risen to a success far beyond anyone's expectations; especially her husband's. And she did not even let him do her accounts. She was, after all, an intelligent woman and her mother had seen to it that she was well educated. She ran her own bank accounts in a separate bank from William's, and employed her own accountant. Every cent went back into the expansion of her business. Only from the market did she take the earnings for pocket money. This small sum made her personally independent. In every other way her husband managed the household finances. Cleo accepted this because she believed that she had brought nothing but herself to the marriage. Perhaps for a long time she had not recognised her own worth. To give her husband credit, he had certainly recognised her value and indeed loved her very deeply. He simply thought he needed to control her life for her. Perhaps he was not confident of his *own* worth. He had succeeded in creating a super, confident businesswoman who had gleaned from him all the "do's" and "do not's". He dealt with this phenomenon of his wife's business success by remaining out of sight, as often as possible, from her guests or clients. He could not praise her, even though he was proud of her.

Ann arrived breathless at Cleo's door and was shown into her office. It was comfortably furnished as a sitting room, with a desk facing the window and a lovely peaceful view of their back garden.

"Sit down, Ann. I'll get some coffee. Have you had lunch?"

"I just came round to see if you had any Magic Butter for Tracy's eczema. George was supposed to buy it this morning from you."

"I gave it to Carly. She came by and helped for a while. I like Carly!"

"Oh dear!" Ann smiled ruefully. "I didn't check with Carly. I left the house in rather a rush. I was a bit annoyed. If you are having lunch now, I'll go on back home. I shouldn't have run out like that."

"Come into the kitchen with me, Ann. See what I brought back from the market." Ann followed Cleo into her extremely well appointed kitchen. On the pristine granite counter top she saw a beautifully made English style veal and ham pie, temptingly cut in slices on a plate. Next to it in a cut glass bowl was a crisp salad.

"I had just finished making the salad when you arrived. Please take time and eat with me. I could do with some company."

What hungry person could resist such an invitation? Ann smiled gratefully and accepted. She watched Cleo cut up a fresh baked loaf. "My husband baked it this morning," she acknowledged, as they carried the necessary things into Cleo's office.

"I like to eat in here. It's entirely private." They ate in silent enjoyment.

Then Cleo said: "I saw George briefly in the market this morning. He seemed a bit agitated; more so than usual, that is." She waited for Ann's response.

"It's because he has nothing to do," Ann said carefully. Cleo waited again. Ann continued. "He used to do a lot of translating of papers and articles for a monthly journal, but that seems to have dropped off lately, which means he gets restless and somehow secretive."

"He has a pleasant nature, though, doesn't he? He's also quite happy go lucky."

"Oh yes," agreed Ann. "I also know that he is a good and honest man and he cares very much for us as a family. But . . ." Cleo waited once more. "Well, he's become, over the years so . . . well . . . useless!" Ann looked horrified by what she had just said. "Oh! I take that back. I didn't mean it." Tears welled in her eyes.

Cleo laid a comforting hand on Ann's. "He just needs something to get his teeth into. I'm pretty sure he has an awful lot to give."

Ann nodded wordlessly and after a moment she spoke again. "I think he needs a break. I think he needs to do something that will make him feel capable, worthy. I wish he would go away and do it and come back when he's worked it out. I am a fairly straightforward person and I don't really understand or appreciate his complications. Financially it makes no difference if he's there or not. Of course, the girls might get fewer treats. He's always good like that. And we'd miss his cooking. He enjoys cooking. Oh my God! What am I talking about?" Ann began to cry in earnest.

"Listen, Ann. You know it does you good to talk. It unravels things for you. Now you've brought those thoughts out into the open, I'm sure something will come of it. You'll see."

Ann dried her tears on a tissue from her pocket.

"Oh Cleo, you always say the right thing. I do feel better now. That was a lovely lunch. I'm glad I came." Ann raised her head and stood up with a crooked smile. "I'll go home now." Cleo gave her a hug.

Ann left Cleo's house in a much better mood. She was positively happy by the time she arrived home and a wild idea had been germinating in her head.

"Hello! Anyone home?" she called into the quiet house as she let herself in. The girls responded with halloos from various corners of the house. The sound of the lawn mower from the back garden told her that George was doing penance for his sins. She leaned out of the back door and beckoned him in.

"I've got an idea." George sat carefully down on a kitchen chair and looked at her warily.

By the time Ann had expounded her plan George was furious. He could neither express nor understand his rage. He stood up and paced from room to room until Ann had to ask him to say something.

"I don't know what to say!" he shouted. Ann was taken aback.

"What's wrong?" she asked.

"I'll tell you what's wrong," he spat vindictively and unfairly. "Last night you said you were going to leave with the kids, and now you are telling me to get out." He paced some more. "You've decided, haven't you? This marriage is over. Kaput! Fini! Pasta!"

"I don't remember saying anything like that," Ann said, genuinely surprised. "Last night *you* said that it was a wonder I didn't leave *you*. I said that there were times when I wished you'd pull your weight but I didn't say I was leaving. You were in a mood of self-recrimination brought on by your own ineptitude. You must have been feeling guilty or something and I really can't help that."

"What do you want me to do for heavens sake? Do you want me to leave or not?"

"No," Ann said carefully. "I don't want you to leave." George's expression was so stricken that Ann took pity on him. "Listen, George. Listen carefully. I suggest that we *all* go to Europe for three weeks. You look into going to the Czech Republic with Edda and that what's-her-name and help them find her family. I will go to France with Carly and Tracy. I have three weeks vacation owing to me to be used before the year's end. Tracy has finished school and is literally hanging about doing nothing. It won't hurt Carly to take a winter break from school to come and visit her aunts in France for two weeks or so. We haven't seen my sisters for two years now. You can join us there for a few days at the end and maybe we'll fly back together."

"What about Sarah?" George sounded mollified.

"Sarah is at university so she won't be involved."

"Ann, you are a saint. I don't deserve this."

"Shut up!" she exclaimed, exasperated. But when he came and put his arms around her, she did not draw away.

Edda spent most of Sunday on the Internet. She typed e-mail letters to her friends in the Czech Republic, announcing her intentions to visit. She did not go into much detail about her mission, but was interested to know what their response would be at her arrival with two friends in tow. She corresponded regularly with many of her old students and had warm friendships with at least three. She could not do any more until she met up again with Ofelia when they hoped to have a more practical discussion of their plan of action. There was a lot to be done before they raced off on a wild goose chase into the heart of Europe. While mulling these things over in her mind, she received a cryptic phone call from George:

"Edda?"

"Yes!"

"Are you meeting at three with Ofelia?"

"Yes!"

"At your house?"

"Yes!"

"See you. Bye." And the phone went dead. Edda looked at the receiver in surprise and then, with a shrug, replaced it. *I wonder what George thinks he's doing?* he wondered briefly. She collected everything she could find from her visit to the Czech Republic and spent a most pleasant hour going over the maps and photographs of Prague. What a memorable city that was, what a beautiful and unspoilt city! One of Prague's most remarkable features was that it had not been devastated in the Second World War. Hitler had seen that it was preserved and protected, for his own use, of course. No matter the reason, thank God it was still so perfect. Edda felt a yearning to be there again.

She had taught at a school within a large automobile parts factory in the small town of Novy Jicin in Moravia, near the Polish border. She hoped her students would rally round her now though whether they would be compelled by Ofelia's story or not, she could not guess.

Time passed. Edda managed a short walk in the park after lunch and soon it was time for Ofelia to arrive. It was cool, so Edda lit a fire in her living room and laid out the tea things. She wanted to create an atmosphere that would allow them to relax and be confident about the enterprise they were about to embark upon. The doorbell rang and she ran to open the door. It was George.

"George! I was expecting Ofelia."

"I phoned to tell you I was coming," said he defensively.

"Well, that's all right. Come on in." She sent him into the living room and fetched an extra cup.

"You'd better get some small glasses," instructed George. "I've brought some Slivovitz. It's Hungarian but it was the best I could do."

A small alarm went off in Edda's head. What was on George's mind? He didn't *really* think he was coming with them, did he? She hurried back into the kitchen to find some shot glasses. *One shot! Down the hatch and throw the glass into her lovely fireplace. Or maybe that was only in Russia?* On her way back with the glasses the doorbell rang again and this time, thank goodness, it was Ofelia, ten minutes late and not the slightest bit apologetic. Edda beckoned her in and pantomimed with rolling eyes and hand gestures that there was someone already present in her living room with intentions of drinking heavily. Ofelia loved intrigue and was willing to forgive any interruption unless it was Ian. Ofelia caught on immediately when she saw George.

"You've come to encourage us and wish us well. To toast our journey with whatever you've got there. How nice of you!"

"Partly true," he admitted. He took the glasses from Edda's outstretched hand.

"Perfect!" George poured three measures and handed them round carefully.

"Now!" He raised his glass to them. Everyone clinked glasses. There was a definite sense of occasion. "Na zdrave!" cried George in a beautiful rolling accent, thrilling Ofelia to her toes and reminding Edda of happy evenings with her friends Petr and Vera. "To your health!" and he downed his drink in one gulp.

Ofelia did the same. Not wishing to be a laggard Edda threw hers back as well. The fiery liquid burned its way down her throat causing the well remembered warm glow to travel all through her chest.

"Na zdrave!" she gasped and everyone laughed.

"So, what's the plan?" George poured himself another shot.

An uncomfortable silence reigned. Edda eyed Ofelia anxiously. George had gatecrashed the party yesterday and now without a by your leave was assuming to be a part of it all. Ofelia appeared to be summing him up. The imposition appeared enormous to Edda. Besides, his wife would surely never agree. Ofelia took a deep breath, studying George intently.

"Milatchku," she breathed. George blushed deeply. "You understood, didn't you?" Ofelia almost screeched. "You understood! What does it mean?"

"It means 'Darling'." George blushed again as he spoke.

"I knew it! I knew it! I *do* come from Czechoslovakia." She burst into tears, and flung herself towards George, planting a big kiss on his cheek and turning just as suddenly towards Edda and kissing her too.

"You two are the most important people in my life at the moment and I love you both immensely," she said, wiping her eyes on her sleeve.

Edda was slightly disconcerted but George looked very satisfied. Apparently he was in on the adventure after all.

Three hours later, they had discussed and viewed their various positions and were ready and willing to embark upon a search for Ofelia's beginnings. Each was doing this for individual reasons and each was fulfilling a strong personal need.

The situation was serendipitous.

Meanwhile, upstairs, Anthea knew her mother was having some kind of a meeting. She had seen George go in but not Ofelia. She could see George's car in the street below her kitchen window and beneath her feet she could hear some kind of goings on. At least there were voices and plenty of conversation. She never knew how to take George and this was the second time in as many days that he was visiting her mother. She was sure she could hear another voice, female. It had to be Ofelia, she guessed. They were discussing the future, and without her. Yet George was with them. Anthea felt hurt and a little angry. Had she not started it all? Made it possible? Why did she feel so left out; her opinion ignored? And if her mother was starting on one of her mad ideas, she needed to be there to inject a little caution. She struggled a little with her thoughts and came to the conclusion that she would leave them to it and go and read. She fell asleep and was woken some time later by a knock on her downstairs door. She went down to answer it. It was Ofelia.

"Come in," she said only a *little* coolly. She was glad for not being totally excluded from their excitement. "Would you like some tea?"

"No thank you. I have been drinking tea with your mother and her friend George."

Ofelia curled herself up on Anthea's sofa in much the same way that she had done only yesterday on Edda's. "I can't stay long but I wanted to tell you what has happened."

Anthea sat opposite her and allowed Ofelia to elaborate briefly before interrupting.

"Are you seriously telling me that you have inveigled my mother to go chasing off into the wilds of middle Europe on some kind of a paper chase?"

"Inveigled!" Ofelia cut in. "Inveigled? It was your mother's idea!"

"My mother," Anthea said tersely, "is completely off her head."

"Oh! You surely can't mean that!" Ofelia said, momentarily stalled.

"Well, what I mean is," Anthea subsided a little. "I mean that she is susceptible to off-kilter ideas. She has an over-keen sense of adventure and is feeling dissatisfied with life at the moment. She is likely to be grasping at straws, for something to do. You have to remember, she's getting on. You know, too old for this sort of thing. She can't go gallivanting at this stage of her life. It's too dangerous." Anthea observed Ofelia closely now. She could see her turning this information over in her mind.

"I think," Ofelia said slowly. "I think that you are *scared* for your mother. Is that what it is? You are afraid that she is biting off more than she can chew and that she won't be able to cope." Anthea sat unnerved as Ofelia read her mind. Ofelia continued. "You think that coping with a teaching position was easy enough because your mother had a secure position and somewhere to live in a foreign country, but now, you think she is taking a step into the unknown; perhaps into danger. Also," she went on mercilessly, "she is going with me, a completely unknown person who you have no reason to trust." As Anthea drew breath to respond, Ofelia said: "Not that my last comment is your first concern, I know, but whoever I am, you don't want your mother led into possible danger unnecessarily."

"Right!" Anthea managed to say.

"After all, you have your only brother in danger in Afghanistan and with your mother off on a similar gig; you would be left on your own with no one. I don't blame you for feeling that way."

"You are a strange girl, Ofelia. How old are you?"

"I'm said to be twenty five by now. I was given an official third birthday on the date of my discovery in the park at Morton Street. I'm probably a few months older though. My only concern about age is that when I turn one hundred, I will already be one hundred, if you see what I mean!" She giggled.

Anthea shook her head and could think of no way to bring the conversation back to a sensible level. She would have to approach her mother about her concerns after Ofelia left.

"Look, nothing is finalised. And anyway, the Czech and Slovak Republics are not dangerous places to be. You . . . ." But Anthea cut her off.

"It's all right. Please don't say any more. I do thank you for coming to *tell* me about your plans." Here Anthea laid slight emphasis upon the word. "But I'd rather not discuss it now if you don't mind. I don't want to be rude or negative, but I do need to be on my own for a while."

She got up and Ofelia did too. At the top of the stairs, Ofelia turned for a final word. "Today is the end of an era in my life. You are the catalyst, which brought this about, Anthea. You are the first person at the beginning of my new life. I thank you for this." She reached out a hand and gently touched Anthea. With a radiant smile she was gone.

On Sunday evening, Edda phoned Cleo, and as a consequence, Cleo phoned Ann. This resulted in the three women meeting for a drink at the "Tipsy Tern". The place had its usual crowd. It was busy but Tommy, the owner, came out for a brief visit and brought them some complimentary nibbles.

"What are you doing working on a Sunday evening, Tommy?" Edda asked.

"I just popped in to fetch something but I got roped in. I've only been here a while. I'm going home. What are you drinking?" He ordered up another round and left with a friendly wave. The women got down to brass tacks.

Cleo brought the meeting to order. "I feel that we should start with Ann. We need to know what role George will play in this adventure."

"Well, I am amazed that everything is falling into place so simply," Ann began. "This has come at a time when if something hadn't changed, I think I would have left, although George may not have realized this. I have to say that even so, I did not want to break up our marriage. But I guess I was on my way. I'd had enough."

Here Cleo thought it wise to interrupt. "I think it's safe to say that we all have a soft spot for him. He has a heart of gold, but then, we don't have to live with him," she added practically.

Ann let out a spurt of laughter.

"Too right!"

"He has always seemed very practical and helpful to me," Edda offered. "I'm just not sure if it's the right thing to take him off with us to the Czech Republic."

"But you see, you say 'take him off.' You don't say 'go away together,'" Cleo pointed out.

"True," Edda noted. "But none the less! What do you think Ann?"

"I have always known that George goes where he wants and does what he likes. I have also always known that he is loyal and loves his family and would do anything to preserve it. If he goes with you it will be on a genuine quest. You, Edda, must also have your own reasons for going. It's not as if you sought him out to come with you, is it? You have to decide for yourself what you feel about taking him with you."

"True," Edda repeated with a smile. "I like George. I think it could be an asset having him with us. Can he really speak Czech?"

"No, not really, nor Slovak," said Ann. "I think he can understand it a bit. He'll be ahead of you and Ofelia for sure. Slovak and Czech are a little different, but I believe they sound much the same and are mutually understandable."

"How's Anthea taking it?" Cleo asked.

"Not very well," Edda said. "She thinks I'm jumping off into something out of my depth."

"You probably are. But you can swim, can't you?"

"Yes. And I want to. It may seem crazy, and possibly immature, but I'd love to feel out of my depth right now. I'm not ready to give in yet. Life hasn't become any clearer. I don't know *why* I'm here but I know there's a reason to be alive and I can only think that it is to live. For the longest time now I have felt that I wasn't truly living or really experiencing life. Do you think I'm crazy?" she asked.

"No," said Ann. "I envy you that feeling."

"I encourage you," said Cleo. "Do whatever you can. You've probably got at least thirty years to do it."

"We all have more to give than we realise. There are too many wasted lives and wasted years." Ann spoke wistfully. Now it was Cleo's turn for reflection.

"Life is never wasted while you are with children. But this won't get us anywhere. Tell us about Ofelia. She just turned up out of the blue. It's uncanny."

"I know," Edda agreed. "But the moment she came in my front door I knew something was going to change. There's no going back, at least that's how it feels."

"Tell me about how Anthea met her. George said Anthea knocked Ofelia's boyfriend down in the street. That doesn't sound like Anthea."

Ann was curious to hear more about this girl who was having quite a disruptive effect on all their lives. Edda spoke of Anthea's meeting with Ofelia on the way to market and recounted as much of Ofelia's memories of before her adoption by the Kingsley family as she felt permissible. It was altogether an extraordinary story, but Edda gave only the bare bones.

Eventually the three women found themselves talking about their shared history. Cleo and Edda had met over twenty years ago when they were both new immigrants. Cleo had been married for five years and was having a hard time dealing with her life, and Edda had been instrumental to Cleo's change of attitude and subsequent emergence to success. Edda had been around to hold her hand when she was afraid her new business, Starkers, would not get off the ground and when her husband had been inclined to sneer. Their friendship went deep and they trusted each other. Ann had entered the picture twelve years ago. Cleo had read Ann's advertisement for a nanny to look after her three small girls and had recommended one of her young employees. They had met and their friendship had grown from there, with Edda soon meeting Ann as well. The trio had spent a lot of time together over the intervening years. One of their best meeting places was at Ann and George's house where George was in his element preparing gourmet meals for what he fondly called his other beautiful women, his wife and three daughters being the first. They were all close-knit in a way that certainly allowed Ann to trust either of her friends with her husband. She also knew that the responsibility of their behaviour lay with the two women. George was altogether too malleable. But the seeds he sowed were mostly the seeds of discontent in Ann's mind.

Edda lay sleepless in her bed that night. The least of her problems was arriving penniless in the Czech Republic. She had a pension to fall back on.

No, the part that unsettled her was not knowing how to go about unearthing Ofelia's past when they arrived. They had absolutely nothing to go on. Here was a girl, ever so slightly "other-worldly," with no past whatsoever before being found wandering in a Toronto park at the age of three. Surely the authorities could have identified her language and checked with Immigration among the Czechoslovakian community in the city? She wondered if Ofelia had already gone down that route. Edda tossed and turned some more. *What if they arrived in Europe and found no trail to pick up? This seemed very likely. I mean, where would anyone begin? And would it be left all up to her?* She visualised George making merry in the pubs and restaurants with new friends and cheap beer.

And Ofelia, did she have financial backup to support this project of hers?

Edda reflected upon her own idiocy. What kind of a woman was she? Several friends had called her brave when she had first announced her decision to go and teach abroad two years ago. Many people thought that the Czech Republic was dangerous.

"And why," they had asked, "would she want to leave the security of her friends and family in Canada?"

Little did they realise that it was fear itself that chased her away from "security." Fear of stagnation; fear of never doing the things she had planned to do in her lifetime; fear of death coming before she had seen the places she wanted to see. Fear drove her forth. She didn't feel brave, but there was something to be said for acting upon her fears in a positive way. Maybe she was not such a fool after all!

Edda fell into a fitful sleep and found herself running wildly with a team of yelping dogs at her heels, into an untamed beautiful country where she was greeted with joy and welcome by all. Eventually she discovered that she was not running but travelling in a chariot drawn by some kind of dragon. A driver, an angelic figure of a man, told her that he was bringing her home to her two sisters who had long been awaiting her arrival.

Ofelia listened to her answering machine. She was waiting for a reply from her mother. There were three messages from Ian, each more desperate than the last. She would have to deal with the matter soon or he would be round on her doorstep again, or more likely in her apartment, because he still had the key. *Why didn't her folks call?* She dialled their number. There was no reply. Much as she relied on the fates coming to her rescue, even she could see that it would be useful to arrive in her native land with *some* clue as to where to begin. A knock on the door deepened the frown on her forehead. If that was Ian . . . she ran to the door and flung it open. It was her mother and father. She beamed in relief.

"Come in. Come in. Did you find the records?" They had promised to dig out the papers she had arrived with and to try and find out the best place to start asking questions.

She had been a child with no background. She had started with a clean slate and Elizabeth and Stan Kingsley had accepted her wholeheartedly. They were not so keen on this latest project of their adopted daughter. Better let sleeping dogs lie, they thought. Who knows what had been going on in middle Europe in those last days of communism? And Mary, as they tended to call her still, had possibly come from a communist block country. This much they had established that very morning with a phone call to Toronto.

"We have a little news for you," said Elizabeth. "They weren't willing to say too much over the phone but you can make an appointment, bring all your information, and I think they'll do their best to help."

"They did say, however," Stan added in his grave and serious manner, "that twenty years ago it was quite possible for refugees to arrive unofficially, which could have led to your mysterious discovery."

"Pshaw!" Ofelia snorted. "Twenty years ago and all the way up to today too." She wasn't sure whether to raise her hopes or not.

"So, what do you think?" she asked tentatively and rather unthinkingly, as it brought her father's opinion right to the fore.

"I think, since you ask," he said, taking advantage of a rarely given opportunity, "that this is a foolhardy endeavour, and that you are setting yourself up for major disappointment. Not only that but you are involving an innocent woman in her fifties . . ."

"Sixties," amended Ofelia.

"Sixties!" her startled father gasped. "A woman in her *sixties*?"

"Well, nearly sixty-one." Ofelia decided to cut this line of conversation short, and asked,

"So! Did you make me an appointment?"

"No, we couldn't do that," her mother answered. "But here's the number and extension and the name of the person we spoke to. She was very nice and helpful. You are to call her after two today." Ofelia glanced at her watch.

"But it's only eleven o'clock," she wailed. "Why do I have to wait so long?"

"Don't be impatient," Stan advised and added tritely, "You've waited twenty-two years. You can wait another hour or two."

"Let us know how it goes, dear. Are you sure you don't want us to come with you?"

"Yes, I'm sure, Mom. I will be all right and I'll tell you every detail when I get back. Okay?"

Her parents drank their tea and left.

Appointment in Toronto

Ofelia arranged an appointment with Toronto's social services. Edda accompanied her. They drove in Edda's car, singing every song they knew. They were very high-spirited.

Ofelia discovered from her records that she had been found, as she had said, wandering in the park in a state of ill health. She had spoken one or two words, which were identified as either Russian, Polish, or some other Slavonic language, and they had searched ineffectively to find a connection with other refugees who were seeking asylum at the time from Eastern Bloc countries. No one had laid claim to her so they had kept vigilance for as much time as they deemed fair before putting her up for adoption, thereby ensuring that she could have the best possible chance for a good restart to her life. Ofelia could not fault them for that, but she was distressed about the gap between a loving father of whom she had a distinct picture in her mind and the fact of her abandonment. She could not reconcile this with her faith in her father's genuine love. He could not have left her. Something must have gone horribly wrong. Edda was intrigued. They went over and over it in the car on the return journey, with no singing this time.

Eventually they came up with a rather wonderful conclusion. They decided that she must have been put in the care of people who had been paid by Ofelia's father to look after her. When she had become ill, they had taken her to the park and left her there where they hoped she would be found and looked after.

"And I think he came back for me and found me gone. I hope he killed that person who deserted me," Ofelia cried fiercely.

"Ofelia! You don't mean that," Edda admonished.

"Maybe not. But I feel that he might have wanted to if he loved me and I was gone." Edda squeezed her hand.

"Of course he would have been devastated to find you gone," Edda agreed, adding, "If that's what happened."

"I think it's possible. And then he would have searched and searched and made inquiries to see if I had been found."

"Perhaps he discovered that you had been found and were safe."

"You mean and then *left* me?" Ofelia was shocked.

"Perhaps," Edda said slowly. "Perhaps he was here without papers and had smuggled you into Canada for this very purpose; to give you a better life." Silence reigned while Ofelia absorbed this. Eventually, when Edda glanced at her, she saw tears rolling down Ofelia's face.

"I would have preferred to be with him." Edda drove on in silence and let her cry.

Edda's thoughts wandered. The theory they had evolved was feasible, but if Ofelia's father had wanted this freedom and better life for his daughter, why had he left her no clues of her identity? Why would he want that? What had had happened to her birth mother? So many questions. But Edda had regained her confidence and was enthusiastic about travelling on this madcap adventure. She had met with George privately and they had frankly discussed the financial angle. George, she was relieved to discover, had ample holiday allowance for this trip. He was far better off than she was. Luckily the cost of living in the Czech Republic was low. Although the country was a member of the European Union, it would still take a few years to become economically caught up. Edda would be able to hold her own. But she must discover what Ofelia intended to contribute. So far she had not found a congenial opportunity.

Moments later, Ofelia broached the subject herself.

"It's going to cost a fair bit to make this trip, even if we manage to find some reasonable fares," she began.

"True."

"I have been wondering at the willingness of you and George to accompany me. I know that you both have connections with that part of the world, and I understand and truly appreciate your excitement for me. But I blindly assumed that it was *my quest* that challenged us to leave Canada on a whim. When I stop to think about it logically I realise exactly how presumptuous I have been," she ended lamely. "I think I'm trying to say that I have involved you in something you should never, never have agreed to."

"I have to say," Edda commented, "that it certainly was your quest that got us all going. But it seems to me, and I have examined the common sense of it all, that George and I are also in need of a quest. Call it our own Holy Grail. My only concern is that we should each of us have enough money or earning ability to get us through." There! She had said it.

"Oh! No worries," Ofelia said blithely. "I have been saving for this moment all my life." She had that far away gleam in her eye again. I have several thousand dollars stashed away and enough air miles to get me first class to anywhere."

"Oh," Edda said faintly.

"In fact, I suspect that all our air fares to Prague or Bratislava will be covered by my airmiles. You can pay your own airport taxes though." She gave Edda one of her radiant smiles. "You were worried about my finances, weren't you?"

"I was a bit."

"I live simply, and my part-time job covers my apartment expenses and groceries. My savings come entirely from my income as a writer. I write short stories and freelance articles for magazines and journals and I put seventy five percent of that income away without fail. I get good money and have saved a lot in three years of writing professionally. I do a couple of articles a month when I'm on a roll. While we're away I'll manage at least one story, and so I will be quite secure."

"That's wonderful, Ofelia, that you are a successful writer. Though I should have guessed when I think about it. You have a wild imagination!" They both laughed.

"You're pretty wild yourself!" Ofelia added.

Leaving Canada

We flew out on a windy November day. Everyone came to see us off except George's family who had already left for France. Anthea was there, looking worried. Even Tommy from the Tipsy Tern brought his wife and four airplane-mad boys. Of course, my beautiful adopted family were there too, Mom and Dad and two of my big brothers, Dave and Ed, who had to see with their own eyes their little sister set off on her big adventure. I told them I'd write every bit of it down. My other brother, Richard living now in England, would certainly have been here too if he could have. Ian was noticeably absent as he had been well and truly dismissed from my life. So this is the first page of my new story. (Written in a style that will keep my brothers reading!)

With these words Ofelia began at once to keep a record of their journey. She figured she'd get a novel out of it, she told her companions; one for her brothers, and, the rewrite for the general public.

"What do you mean the rewrite?" questioned George from his comfortable business class seat on the Czech Airline jet from Toronto.

"I mean that I'll be writing in a special way for my illiterate brothers and a proper, serious book for my general public." George glanced at Edda, who shook her head and smiled reassuringly at him.

"It's all right George," she said. "It's just the way she and her brothers interact. They are quite literate actually. I've met them."

"Oh," George said, reaching for his Slivovitz. He noticed Edda's faint look of distaste. Hoping it was for the drink and not for him, he commented, "You haven't got used to the idea of this yet! But you will!" He actually smirked. "Slivovitz will oil the way for us in our enquiries, you'll see."

"I hope you aren't going to drink your way through this trip," Edda spoke tartly. George frowned. He knew he liked to drink and that where they were going the booze was going to be so readily available it was almost indecent not to make a habit of it. He also knew that this was his chance to redeem himself in his own eyes. To make something of himself; to prove that he was, after all a capable and responsible human being. This was his time to make his family proud of him. So he promised himself right there that he and his drinking habits would maintain a casual but friendly relationship. There was a great deal to be said for enjoying a social drink without going overboard. George spent some time going over all this with himself. He gave himself a good talking to.

Edda was beside herself with pleasure at the luxury. She had never been able to travel this way before and up until now the destination had been more important than the actual journey. Now she wasn't so sure. It was not only the comfort of the seating; the fact that one could stretch out and lie flat which prevented the strain of sitting with the aching she usually experienced after a trans Atlantic flight, but also the thoughtful service and the feeling that the attendants had time to look after you. Edda wondered if she could ever bear to travel tourist class again. It would be akin to riding in a cattle truck!

The attendant offered her champagne with her dinner. She accepted it graciously. By the time they prepared for landing, Edda had been asleep for five hours out of the eight on the flight to Prague; something never before experienced in all the flying she had done in the last forty years.

Ofelia put her writing away and stretched. She loved travelling business class. Any moment now she would set foot onto the soil of her homeland and she wondered how she would feel. She was now a worldly young Canadian woman; educated and confident. What had she been when she left twenty-five years ago? She dozed and her mind wandered.

Time suddenly telescoped and with amazing speed, the small, frightened child arose gasping from within her. She heard an explosion. Red hot and deafening, but strong arms held her securely. "Tati! Tati!" She screamed and awoke, amazed to find she had not screamed aloud. Her ears were still ringing.

"Tati!" she murmured.

"Mm?" George queried politely. The seatbelt lights were on and they were preparing to land. The plane was circling the rooftops of Prague.

Edda awoke at this point, refreshed and full of anticipation. Ofelia reached out and grasped her hand tightly. She smiled bravely at Edda, her lips tightly pressed together. On Edda's other side, George, to her surprise, had a tear rolling down his face as he drank in the sight of the red roofs below.

Well, here we are, Ofelia thought. *Let the Adventure begin.*

Part II

The Czech Republic

Edda, who managed the itinerary, had booked them into a small central hotel because they had expressed the desire to explore the ancient city. They decided to make time for at least two days of sightseeing, both for recuperation after the flight and to familiarise themselves with the newness of it all. It was late morning now, so Edda suggested a stroll to try to adapt as quickly as possible to the time zone. They felt fine enough at the moment but back in Toronto it was about four a.m.

They turned towards the Vltava River, wandering through Stare Mesto, the Old City, along the cobbled streets and through countless tiny passages. They were seeking the famous Charles Bridge. The weather was cold with a nip of frost in the air. People, well wrapped up, were walking fast to keep the cold out. Slim women smartly dressed and wearing high heels, managed the cobbled sidewalks with practised ease. They emerged from the streets to see the ancient bridge before them.

"Karluv most," breathed Ofelia, who had been doing her homework.

"That's right!" Edda said, almost proud to be the one to introduce them to their city, which she so loved, "The Charles Bridge."

It was a wide bridge, long closed to vehicular traffic, and pleasantly uncrowded with fewer tourists about at this time of year. They walked slowly across, taking in the broad river. On top of the hill on the far bank the castle stood proudly overlooking the city. The Renaissance bell tower of the cathedral of Saint Vitus loomed behind it, and below it lay Mala Strana, the Little Quarter, sprawled in a maze of cobbled streets and steps climbing raggedly to the top. "We'll walk up there if you like," offered Edda.

"I hope we can get a coffee first," George said, an expression of alarm on his face.

"I know just the place," she said, grinning. "Let's all go and touch the statue of Saint John first. Ask him for success in our search."

In the centre of the bridge, among the statues lining the parapet on both sides was the oldest one: Saint John of Nepomuk. To touch him was to ensure your happy return to Prague. His four-hundred year old foot, pointing downwards and just within reach, had been polished to a shine by hundreds of hopeful hands. Ofelia, Edda and George touched his foot together. Energy seemed to course from the statue through them. They exchanged mystified smiles and continued on their way.

There is nowhere like Prague. Prague is special. To enter from Canada or the U.S. or even from Britain is to walk into one of those fairy tale cities once read about in stories and seen in the child's mind's eye. It was already casting its spell on them.

Edda led them to a delightful café below the bridge. After an excellent coffee, they managed the strenuous climb up to the castle. There was so much to take in that they simply sauntered, climbed and wondered. They ambled through the precincts of the cathedral and castle, admiring the golden window and the statue of Saint George killing his dragon. They observed the blue-clad solemn guards standing silently at attention, oblivious of visitors' interested stares and they noted that the President of the Czech Republic was present in his castle. Eventually, having wound their way down again through various palace gardens to the streets below, tired now and hungry too, they retraced their steps across the Charles Bridge.

The trio turned into a warm little restaurant and found a table by the window. They hung their coats on a coat rack and the waiter was at their side before they were seated. He wished them good day in English, handing out menus and asking what they would like to drink.

"*Pivo, prosim.*" Edda ordered in her best Czech. "*Dvakrat malova a jena velkovo.*" She knew it wasn't perfect but she just couldn't resist the temptation to roll the old familiar words from her tongue; they were faultily put together but the waiter smiled at her genially, and bowed.

"*Dobra! Dobra!*"

"*Mate Staropramen?*" she asked jauntily.

"*Ano*," he said, and repeated the order slowly and correctly so she could both hear the words and be able to confirm her order.

"Wow!" said Ofelia, who thought that Edda and the waiter had had a full conversation. "That was impressive. What have you ordered?"

"Three local beers!" Edda said with satisfaction. "Small ones for us and a large one for George."

While they waited for the beer, they studied the menu and George enjoyed recognising the old dishes that his mother used to cook for him and his brother as children during their early days in Canada. George fancied the pork, dumplings and sauerkraut, or even tripe soup, (Edda shuddered), and Ofelia was almost keen to try whatever he suggested until she heard the soup's main ingredient, but Edda was strictly set on the salmon. The prices were excellent even for Prague, and Edda explained that this particular restaurant, which she had frequented in early days when visiting the city, was a "Czech kitchen", and that meant that the citizens of Prague ate here. It was not a tourist spot.

"This is great," said George. What a team we're going to make. Na zdravi!"

"Na zdravi!" said all three as they clinked their glasses in friendly accord and the waiter came forward smilingly to take their orders.

Somehow, those few days in Prague relaxed and prepared them for the task ahead. George began to find his feet. It became obvious that he could not speak the language, but he clearly had an affinity with it, and unlike Edda, to whom the Slavic tongue was so unfamiliar and difficult to learn, he slid into a form of communication that rapidly improved along with his vocabulary.

Ofelia, in the first flush of pleasure at being in Prague, where she firmly believed she should be, was fleetingly overcome with shock at the realisation of what this would mean both to herself and her adopted family if her quest were successful. She was filled with chagrin at the thought of exchanging the family that had chosen her, for a new and unknown family in this country, who, if they even existed, might have no place left for her today. *Am I a fool on a wild goose chase?* she wondered wistfully. *Am I riding roughshod over the feelings of my Canadian mother and father and brothers?* She knew she loved them and was not ungrateful, but the ever present drive to find her roots overcame all of it. She sent her love to them in Canada over the ether.

The Prague weather took a turn for the better. The wind stopped and the sky shone a brilliant blue. They explored not only the castle and famed streets of Mala Strana below it, but also Petrin hill with its little Eiffel tower and the magical Hall of Mirrors. They watched with fascination, the march of time, as the six-hundred year old astronomical clock tolled the hour from Starometska Radnice, the Old City Hall. They drank a beer or two in the *U Krale Brabant,* supposedly Prague's oldest pub, which they discovered on one of the hilly alleys coming down from the castle. The entrance led into a smoky basement churning with the hubbub of conversation and muted laughter. The tantalising aroma of hot mead mingling with roasted pork was enough to make even the vegan Ofelia's mouth water. Dim yellow lamps lit the vaulted cellar and ancient swords pierced the centre of the rough oak tables. Rough fur pelts rested on the back of the wooden benches while a group of leering skulls stared at them from a dark corner of the ceiling. It was like stepping into medieval times.

On her last night in Prague, Ofelia dreamt she was standing on the edge of a very high cliff, with white fluffy clouds skudding gently in the sky overhead. As she looked out to sea the overwhelming sensation was one of power. She felt she could fly.

All good things must come to an end and on the third day they packed and set off by metro to the bus station. The ride to Novy Jicin was uneventful. They travelled the one and only highway across the country to Brno, the second largest city in the country, which scarcely attracted much interest from the rest of the world but nonetheless held much of the ancient charm of all Czech cities. Here they changed buses and had only a short wait for their connection to Novy Jicin. The whole journey took about five hours.

"Could have got back to Canada in that time," Ofelia observed, yawning hugely in the Novy Jicin bus station as Edda hailed a taxi to take them to the little guesthouse she had arranged with the help of her friends in town.

"Ah! Though you wouldn't want to be back home just yet now, would you?" Edda asked.

"Not at all! *This* is beginning to feel like home. I love it so far." Ofelia was overcome with an unexpected attack of nerves. "But, you know, I am starting to feel a little scared too." Edda smiled and gave her a reassuring pat on her shoulder.

"Don't you worry. Things are going to turn out just perfectly. Believe me!"

"I do," Ofelia replied patting her own chest for double reassurance.

The taxi man was reaching for their bags and giving George a dirty look at the same time. George paid no attention. Edda noticed all this and smiled with glee at the familiar sight of the grumpiness of the provincial Czech. She could almost see his thoughts; *Bloody foreigners!* Through the taxi window, Edda indulged in nostalgic reminiscence as they drove through the small medieval city to their destination. They left the bus station and followed a narrow cobbled street to the lovely old square with its four-sided arcades and the pokey little shops inhabiting the four hundred year old buildings like nomads. Time had marched on. Modern signs hung over the doorways jostling the gothic archways, completely indifferent to history. But Edda felt the ancientness of the place and it satisfied a hunger in her. She was somehow nurtured by it, alive, alert and receptive, in the element where miracles happened. This was what was meant by "faith can move mountains." Edda was in a position to move mountains and she knew in her bones, right then and there in that grumpy man's taxi, that they would find Ofelia's father.

In less than five minutes their hosts were greeting them, taking their baggage and drawing them into their home. Mr. and Mrs. Novak were a middle aged couple, friendly and effusive for Czechs, completely unable to speak English but occasionally breaking into German as if this might help things along.

They lived in an older house, its stucco exterior painted a glowing apricot. It stood in a pretty garden on the edge of the River Jichinka. The Novaks led their guests up the broad stairway to their rooms, where they found themselves overlooking the bubbling waters of the stream. George had the smaller room and Ofelia and Edda were to share a larger one.

The sheets were sparkling white and folded back with a fluffy down-filled duvet on the end of each bed. Fresh flowers, still flowering calendula and nasturtiums brought in from the garden filled the rooms with their brightness. The windows were flung open to let in fresh air. Ofelia leaned out to look around. The walls were as thick as if it were a stone house, and gave one a feeling of ageless strength. Their hostess, who had introduced herself as Rosa Novakova, closed the windows to maintain the rooms' warmth now that the guests had arrived. There were lots of thank yous and smiles from the well pleased guests and with a flow of unintelligible Czech, Mr. and Mrs. Novak headed back downstairs.

"What did she mean?" Ofelia asked, looking hopefully from George to Edda.

"I really don't know," Edda said, still grinning happily.

"Me neither," said George. "I'm going to unpack a bit, brush up and go down and see what's what," he announced.

"Good idea!" Edda agreed. "And then I'll phone Vera at work and tell her we're here. Come on Ofelia." They dispersed to their quarters and began to settle in. There was a large bathroom on the same landing and apparently no other room but a small box room, which Ofelia checked out. They had the floor to themselves. They made their way downstairs again. The hallway at the foot of the stairs led through an archway to a huge living room where a log fire burned brightly. Mr. Novak had brought in a fresh pile of wood and he smiled and nodded, encouraging them to be seated around the fire. On the coffee table, a tray was laid out with plates and mugs, a jug of warm milk and some interesting looking pastries.

"Ooh! Kolachki! My favourites." Edda's joy was getting out of hand. Mrs. Novakova entered at this point bearing a pot of freshly brewed coffee. It smelt delicious.

"Na! Na!" She gestured encouragingly towards the plate. Edda scooped up a plum tart. It was a palm sized flat soft pastry case filled in the middle with a dollop of heavy plum preserve, more fruit than jam, and tasting like . . . like . . . a waking dream when the memory is sharpest. *This is the Czech life.* She breathed to herself. Outwardly she spoke, speaking through the fruit bursting in her mouth,

"Shvestka!"

"Plums!" echoed George excitedly. "Slivovitz plums!" Both Mr. and Mrs. Novak nodded vigorously in unison.

"'No!' No! Shvestka, slivovice."

"Why are they nodding and saying 'no'?" said Ofelia in a bewildered voice.

"They are actually saying '*ano*', which means 'yes'," George explained patiently. "And '*ne*' means 'no'. You just have to get used to it." He helped himself to an apricot kolachki and offered one to Ofelia. "My mother used to make these all the time," he said. "She had to get the especially fine flour from a chef she knew. You can't just buy such finely ground flour over the counter in Canada." George grew reflective.

Maminka had been a strong minded woman, ruling the roost at home, and although his father had been the one to drop bombs over Nazi Germany, George was sure that maminka had put him up to it. The family had emigrated from Austria before George could remember but he certainly recalled those early days in Toronto with maminka in the kitchen, slapping their hands away as he and his older brother Johnny reached for the cooling Christmas cookies on the rack.

"Leave them!" she would scold in Slovakian, "I must decorate first. Then only can you taste."

But the kolachki now, they were an everyday affair and would be served for breakfast or a snack.

"This is what we eat in the old country." She would boast, "I get flour from Slovak baker on the Danforth. Only he has the fine, fine flour you need for these kolachki."

George's family had moved to Guelph and managed to buy a large roomy house, which his mother turned into a lucrative home for the aged. The baking stopped and the rooms of the house were filled with needy old folk who required all her care and expertise. George recalled a time when there were no bedrooms left, and he and Johnny had slept on a mattress under the dining room table. It was about this time that their father seriously took to drink. These were his childhood years and memories. Now with Mrs. Novakova's pastries melting in his mouth, he became a four year old again.

Mrs. Novakova was pleased with her guests. She poured coffee, asking each of them in turn, "S mlekem?" With milk? Edda translated for Ofelia. George grasped any words pertaining to childhood; nurturing words. Ofelia had noticed that whereas their hostess had introduced herself with a longer name that had sounded to Ofelia's ears like "Vakova", her husband had held out his hand and said, "Jan Novak." She asked Edda about it. Edda explained that when a woman took the name of her husband in marriage as in the case of Rosa, she was virtually calling herself Rosa of Novak, which translated to Rosa Novak-ova. Ofelia pulled a wry face. She was not sure she liked the possessiveness of that.

"What about the children?" she asked.

"Well the boys are like the father and the girls add 'ova' I'm afraid!" Edda laughed at Ofelia's expression of disbelief. So Edda continued, "It's all in the attitude you take you know!" Ofelia gave one of her snorts.

"I suppose I'm going to discover that my name is going to be something—ova, then," she said glumly.

"Very likely," Edda agreed. She disappeared to telephone Vera, leaving Ofelia to mull over the subject of her identity. *Mary Morton, a name plucked out of a hat and pinned on her breast. A simple name, easily changed to Mary Kingsley. And then Ofelia took over. Miss Ofelia Kingsley,*

Mish Ofelia, Myshka Miluchka. George broke in on Ofelia's mulling, his third kolatchki finished.

"Penny for them?" Ofelia regarded him with curiosity and went ahead:

"Milachko means 'darling', doesn't it?" George nodded and smirked. "So what does myshka mean?"

"Well, mysh means mouse. Perhaps myshka is a diminutive of it," he said, hesitantly.

"Little mouse," Ofelia repeated slowly. Then Edda burst in with the news that Vera and Petr were coming to pick them up at five.

"We're invited to supper," she said with satisfaction. As far as she was concerned, life was on a seriously upward trend.

Canada

Back in Guelph, Anthea thoughtfully licked honey off a spoon in her kitchen, overlooking the street below. By now, her mother had been gone over a week and there had been no word. Not one. Her mother had warned her of this, of course. She had said she would be in touch as soon as she arrived in Novy Jicin and have access to the local Internet café or to a friend's computer. She had said it would be at least five days. Well this was day seven. She did not know if she was annoyed or worried. How could anyone's mother be so irresponsible?

She called Ann. Ann wasn't in. Of course not, they had just gone to France to visit relatives. She'd have to call Ofelia's parents. She did not know them well and did not want to appear too ignorant of the situation. Oh well. She should have the telephone number on a pad here by the phone, but it was missing. Where had she put that note pad? She searched a bit and then remembered the file of Czech contacts her mother had given her. This was in her desk drawer and she had probably put the telephone number in that file. She hoped so. Alas, it did not appear to be there. Anthea wandered back into the kitchen, file in hand, and retrieved her chamomile tea. She sipped reflectively, leaning over the sink and peering down to the street. She would have to look up the number in the directory. What was their last name? Oh good grief! For the life of her she could not remember . . . She felt so angry and helpless and her back ached. Peevishly, she blamed her mother, who often left her feeling inadequate. She suspected this was because her mother always bracingly took action when life got her down, whereas she, Edda's daughter, tended to retreat into her shell.

A van pulled up outside. Anthea looked out curiously and recognised one of the Krazy Konstruction Krew vans. One of Ofelia's brothers. He was coming to her house. Which one was it? She couldn't tell them apart. How embarrassing could this get! She ran downstairs and opened her door.

"Hi!" he said. "It's Dave Nelson. Remember me?"

"Of course!" she lied, wondering why his name was Nelson and not Kingsley. "I was just thinking of phoning your parents to see if they had heard anything yet. They are your parents?" she said hesitantly.

"Stan's our step-dad since I was about ten." He smiled reassuringly at her and she looked relieved.

"Do you want to come in?" she invited.

"Sure," he said. "If you don't mind. We could have a chat and exchange news, sort of thing." He tipped his head politely in query.

"Come on up," she said, and rushed nervously up ahead of him.

"I'll leave my shoes down here first. They're a bit muddy because I've just finished work." Anthea offered him a beer, which he accepted. She was glad she had had some in her fridge. There were a couple left over from her brother's last leave from Afghanistan in September. She supposed it would still taste alright.

"Good beer!" he smiled. "Aren't you having one?"

"I'll pour myself a glass of wine," she said, feeling a sudden surge of camaraderie. As she returned with her wine, she noticed him surveying her living room with a look of appreciation. "I like this room," he announced. "It has a comfortable atmosphere." It was a sunny room by day and by night it glowed with golden lamplight. She had leafy plants and a comfortable old settee and armchair both reupholstered in a pattern of birds, with monkeys hiding in jungle greenery. A few brightly coloured cushions were scattered around and on the floor lay an Afghan rug that her brother had brought back. The room had an altogether opulent appearance. Anthea, who had a good old-fashioned streak, loved it.

"I'm glad you like it," she said. "Have you heard from Ofelia, by the way?" she asked as casually as possible.

"Well, no." Dave looked at her earnestly, causing her to feel quite uneasy. "I naturally thought you would have heard from your mother, though. Haven't you?"

"No," she admitted. "Mum's a great promoter of 'no news is good news'. Most annoying at times." She smiled to make light of it.

"Feely probably just wasn't thinking. That would be typical of her. Lovely girl but often completely thoughtless. Probably the result of having three older brothers doing too much for their baby sister! Always thinks someone else will deal with the mundane stuff. Do we have a way of contacting them? She told us that your mother had several addresses where they could be reached in an emergency."

"I don't think their thoughtlessness has reached the emergency level yet," Anthea said seriously. "Though you'd never know, would you?"

"Have you sent any e-mails to anyone yet?" he enquired. "Perhaps you would pass on Edda's or George's and I could whip off a few lines to them. I've got Feely's e-mail of course, but she's not replying. Mum's a teeny bit worried."

"I'm a teeny bit worried myself," said Anthea, "though I should know better by now. Let's look online right now. It's nearly five p.m. here so what's the time in central Europe?" After some mathematical acrobatics they decided that it was nearly eleven p.m. in the Czech Republic.

"But they'll all be in bed by now. My mother says they're early risers." Anthea checked her e-mail quickly. There was nothing from the Czech Republic but there was a note from Ann to Anthea.

> Having a great time in France. It is really great being with my sisters again after so long.
> Have you heard from our adventurers?
> The girls send regards,
> Love from Ann

Anthea and Dave stared at each other, wondering. "No point in worrying. This is typical of all three it would seem," Anthea said reassuringly.

"Sure!" Dave said. "Let's talk about something else!"

"I'll get you another beer," Anthea said. She found that she wanted him to stay a while which was an unusual response for her, but he had an easy way with him and did not make her feel as nervous or threatened as she often all too easily did. She must just make sure not to talk about herself. That would never do. She must keep a respectable distance and that should not be too hard, as she had only just met him for the second time and it was in a spirit of friendship brought about by their adventuring relatives.

Dave had promised to return promptly to his parents with a report of sorts from Anthea if possible, but it was over two hours before he actually left. Anthea discovered that he was separated with two young girls who were with their mother, but came to him on alternate weekends and quite often during the week as well. He maintained a friendly relationship with his ex-wife, which he said made it much easier on the kids. Dave and his ex-wife even shared some family events together quite companionably. "Just so long as I don't have to live with her," he said, his brow darkening. He had been separated for two years already and was happy with his life at last, though it had been tough at first. "Feeling a failure was the worst," he said. Now apparently, he was enjoying his freedom and revived bachelor days. "How about you?" he suddenly asked.

Anthea, to her horror, found herself confessing to a broken marriage from seven years ago. She had been abrupt but he persisted. "No boyfriend since?"

"No!"

"Why not?" The question was searing. Anthea could only stare, keeping her facial expression as neutral as possible. Into the small silence, Dave was the first to speak.

I'm sorry. I shouldn't be so direct. I only meant that I'm surprised that you haven't been snapped up . . . I'm sorry!" he repeated.

"I'm sorry too," she said. "I just don't usually talk much about it. I should make more efforts to find friends." Here the familiar wash of despair overcame her. He asked,

"Maybe you don't get out enough?" She looked at him hopelessly as he started in on her. He guessed immediately that he was being insensitive. "I only meant that you are an attractive girl and that I'd never seen you around before . . ." he stumbled on his words. Something in her expression; an indefinable fearfulness made him realise that perhaps there had been something particular about her divorce that she could not easily share. "Sorry! I should shut up."

"It's all right," she said. "Somehow I can't overcome a certain . . ." Here she hesitated so much that Dave asked gently,

"Is it that you can't trust men any more? Or, should I say, relationships with men?" His head tipped a little to the side again in a gesture she already recognised.

"That would be partly true," Anthea admitted, her head bent and studying the pattern of one of the monkeys on the end of her settee.

"But there is a whole lot more to it than that." Dave actually reached over to where she sat opposite him and picked up her hand. She recoiled, jerking her hand away.

"Something bad happened to you, didn't it?"

"Yes!" she said, and the air had a razor like sharpness in it. "Worse than you can imagine." Anthea's voice made the hairs on the back of Dave's neck stand on end. But he just knew that he had to make her say whatever it was. She seemed to be on the edge of a precipice, continually looking down onto something dreadful that wouldn't go away, locked in like a repeating nightmare.

"Tell me!" he demanded. "Please tell me." And this time he picked up both of her hands and she did not pull away.

"I had a baby." She looked into Dave's eyes. "And my husband killed him." The room went icy cold. Slowly and carefully Dave went down on his knees in front of the stricken girl and pulled her gently into his arms as he had seen his mother do to his young adopted sister Ofelia. After a few seconds she began to cry, quietly at first and then as if her heart would break. They stayed like this for a long time. Eventually, Dave looked down and saw that she had fallen asleep. He gently laid her down on the sofa. He covered her with a nearby shawl, and making a note of her land phone number, he quietly let himself out. It was seven o'clock in the evening and quite dark. He felt much shaken.

Anthea dreamt of walking in a flower garden. Through a rose covered bower she came across a happy group of children, playing in the sunlight. An older girl was skipping, leading a broken circle of children under an archway in the glade's centre. The smaller children were firmly held by the protecting hands of older children. There was much laughter. Anthea advanced and a small boy released himself from the group and came slowly towards her. They stopped, still at a distance, and observed each other. A sweet smile was on the child's face. Anthea's arms reached out wide and her heart stopped. At that moment, an angelic figure swiftly swooped and lifted the boy. Transfixed, Anthea waited. The angel approached, and without letting go, placed the little boy into her heart. She felt such painful joy that she thought she might die. As the angelic being went through her, carrying her precious child, Anthea sank gently into a trance, with the warm imprint of her child in her breast. The sound of bells more strident than music awoke her. It was the telephone ringing at one o'clock in the morning. It was her mother.

"I'm so sorry to wake you, Darling! How do you feel?"

"Stunned."

"What do you mean, Anthea? Look, I would not be calling at this time but Ofelia has been insisting since we got up this morning. It's seven a.m. here. Has something happened?"

"Not really. I'm absolutely fine Mum. Don't worry. I was dreaming," she faltered,

"Oh Mom!"

"Anthea, my darling, what is it? What did you dream?"

"I dreamt that my baby .... Christian ... was all right. It was sad and happy at the same time." Anthea drew a shuddering breath, "I feel better about it. A bit better. Tell Ofelia that her brother Dave came round and we had a good conversation."

Edda drew her own breath of long awaited relief but said nothing. She knew what a strain it was for Anthea to unburden herself, and that she hated a fuss. Anthea rushed on.

"But what about you? We are desperate for news. None of you has sent a peep."

"True dear. Well we had nothing to say other than we are having a great time. The weather is being kind too. I just love it here. We have started looking up the records in Novy Jicin. I don't think that they will tell us much, but they are leading us to people who knew what was going on twenty odd years ago. Ofelia is keeping a running diary on our activities, so nothing of our journey will be lost." Hesitantly, Edda reverted to her daughter's dream. "I'm glad for your dream, Anthea. We *can* talk about it when you're ready? At least now I know that Ofelia was right to make me call you. She's a strange girl sometimes."

"Her brother is nice too," Anthea admitted, enigmatically. "We got on quite well. I'll tell everyone that your quest is more or less going as expected and we'll hear from you again soon."

"All right," said her mother. "We are going to the Internet café this morning, so you can all expect an e-mail. 'Bye Darling! I love you."

"'Bye, Mom. I love you too."

Anthea belatedly got ready for bed. The unspeakable memory of her husband's brutal anger, and his impatience with newborn Christian's endless plaintive crying, and his subsequent behaviour that led to his death had been partly mitigated by her dream. It was out in the open, thanks to Dave. She was at long last staring her pain in the face. She moaned and keened in her sorrow. Though she might never hold her precious baby in her arms again, she knew she would always hold him in her heart. That was where Christian was: in her heart. And she would carry him there for the rest of her life . . . as she moved forward in her life. *Christian, Christian,* she repeated his name softly. I can say your name again. She got slowly into bed, cried a little more, and then sank into one of the deepest sleeps she had had for a long time. She awoke in the morning feeling clear headed and more at ease than she had been for seven years.

But Dave was worried and did not know what to do. He had visited his parents after the episode with Anthea. He had naturally not shared the experience with them, as he felt that this was still a painfully private matter for Anthea and perhaps for her whole family, yet he truly felt he should share the burden with someone wise. What in God's name had her husband done? If Anthea had kept herself from having a life because of this tragic event from her past, someone should help her. But he should not be the one to do it. He found it hard enough to help himself. He was all tied up emotionally and financially with his own family. His daughters were twelve and fourteen and more than enough for him to deal with at the present. His brother would be full of jokes and patronising advice. That was not what he needed. He went home. Ed was still out. Dave made himself a sandwich, had another beer and sat watching television for a while. It bored him silly. He went to bed with a book. He was currently reading Mervyn Peake's *Gormenghast Trilogy,* and he was somehow soothed by the story's elements: the castle city with its host of surreal characters, Swelter the large and sweaty cook, Flay the faithful retainer, Prunesquallor the doctor and observer and Steerpike, the dreadful protagonist, acting in a parody of actual life, life at its most pithy and accurate, and at times harshly fundamental.

As he fell asleep he thought that he might offer the books to Anthea when he was finished. Whatever happened, he would go and see Anthea tomorrow.

He phoned her at eight the next morning. Direct as usual, he said to her: "How are you this morning? I felt it best to leave after you fell asleep but I have been worrying about you ever since. Just worrying that you may be regretting having spoken to me. I had no right to do that to you. I had the strangest compulsion to make you speak. I truly do not know where it came from. I hope you will forgive me.

"Nothing to forgive," she answered. *Oh hell!* Dave thought. *She's gone into denial again.*

"I don't know what happened," she continued, but I feel as if a heavy and painful weight has been removed. I feel better. I feel that I can face the future. I have to thank you for whatever made you get tough with me. I still hurt very much but I think I've let go a bit. I owe you the rest of my story but if you don't mind, not yet."

"No of course not. I am so glad for you and relieved for myself. I would *not* want to be the cause of more pain for you. Yes we'll talk again soon. We must keep in touch about Ofelia whatever happens." And Dave said goodbye. *Whatever happens!* he thought, and went to turn on his e-mail. There was a quick note from Ofelia saying they were all alive and well and that there was nothing yet to report. He noticed that she had forwarded her mail to Anthea as well as the rest of the family and her friends. He presumed that Anthea would check her e-mail eventually. He went off to join his brother who had gone on ahead of him to the job site. Still, inside he felt perturbed about Anthea's story.

The Czech Republic

On that first afternoon in Novy Jicin, they had not known where to start on their search. Edda thought of her former landlord Mirek and his grandfather.

"I've got a lead!" she exclaimed excitedly, after telephoning Mirek. He had relatives who had been up to their necks in conspiracies against the communist regime. His family had fought their invaders throughout history. And now Mirek was arranging a meeting with his grandfather, whom Edda had met previously. He had been a callow youth when Hitler marched in and he had plenty of stories to tell. But it would be his daughter Mirek's mother, that they would now also meet, a widow who just might be able to explain how Ofelia's plight had come about. Ofelia looked scared.

"I almost don't want to know," she said. "I don't want to hear anything bad."

"Since we don't even know who you are," George said, "we are not likely to hear bad news, are we?"

"Right!" said Ofelia with aquiesence. "I wonder what my real name is."

"Probably not Ofelia," he said. Then to Edda, "When is the meeting?"

"Not till tomorrow," Edda said. "They have to give them time to rally around a bit. Mirek told them what it's all about. They don't get as excited as we do about it."

"I wonder why?" Ofelia mused. George spoke,

"Because it is not so romantic for them. This country has lived under oppression for so long, it is all rather grim. Believe me I know. My family were involved in the forties. My father's family fought against Hitler with the Brits after we were smuggled out. I'm looking forward to talking with this old guy you told me about, Edda. I have a weird feeling, being in this atmosphere which I've never experienced for myself, but which my father talked about so much. They just live with it, but to us it is astounding."

Mirek's grandad had previously told Edda stories of his family during the last days of the old Austro-Hungarian Empire and his own dreadful experiences in Nazi occupied Czechoslovakia. He had a wealth of knowledge. His children had grown up under communism, fighting it all the way. This family had a history of subversiveness! If *they* could not set them on the right path, surely no one could.

We'll find out tomorrow," said Edda. "Right now, get your glad rags on because Petr and Vera are cooking fish for us tonight. He's got a big carp. It'll be lovely, and lucky for you George," she added giving him a withering glance, "because he's looking forward to a drinking companion. He too, loves his Slivovitz."

Vera's Petr loved a good time. They lived in an old house left to Vera by her father, and were slowly renovating it. Petr worked very hard. At weekends, he tended to play hard too. This was a Friday night and he was looking forward to seeing them. Petr and Vera were in their early forties. Edda loved them both. They had been the best of friends to her during her teaching year in the Czech Republic, and had accepted her as one of them.

She had met Vera first. Edda had a lesson slot once a week when she was supposed to have a one-on-one with the manager of the Headlights Division at the car plant. Pan Josef Smid never turned up. He always sent his two secretaries instead. Vera and Sharka had been learning English in this way apparently for the last five years. Unhappily, they hadn't picked much up. Edda had set about remedying this with some little progress based heavily on the friendship they soon developed. They had asked her if she ever went out to the pub. Edda admitted she went out on her own to eat sometimes, but not to drink. They immediately took her in hand. She had been here almost two months and was not going out socially! This began her weekly outings and fast friendships. Edda was soon invited to Vera's home where she met Petr, Vera's big-hearted, happy-go-lucky husband. They never made her feel older. They completely disregarded the twenty years difference in their ages and Edda had always marvelled gratefully at their friendship.

This evening they had about a half hour walk ahead of them to their dinner date. All three of them were walking everywhere and already felt the better for it. They stopped in the square at a grocery store, where George bought a large bottle of the dreaded plum brandy. Having heard that Petr liked to drink socially, he had also heard that Vera did not like it when Petr drank too much and that Edda did not want to cause them grief. He planned to be circumspect. Edda bought two bottles of local Moravian red wine. Modry Portugal appeared to be the favourite.

On their way they were accosted by an old gypsy, calling for their attention to his playing. He was in possession of a battered and fairly tuneless old fiddle. Edda recognised him with pleasure from earlier days and called "Ahoy!" He laughed in glee and saluted her before he began. She smiled fondly. He had always been a wicked old fellow. The townsfolk did not like him much nor any of his compatriots for that matter. Czechs largely hated gypsies and were intolerant of them. When the old fellow had played himself out, which did not take very long, George and Ofelia were surprised to see Edda take out a one hundred krona note and give it to him. He smiled and took her hands in his dirty fists and shook them gently.

"*Dekuji, dekuji, dekuji,*" he thanked her three times. Taking a small silver coin from his jacket pocket, he pressed it into her palm, and said something which she did not understand.

"*Dekuji!*" she said in return. As they left, she called back to him in English.

"And don't spend it on cigarettes!" He laughed and waved. He got the "cigarette" part.

Dinner was a lively affair. The evening went well until nine o'clock, when Edda decided that it was time to go home. Vera was tired and they would meet again on Sunday.

"Oh come on!" George said. "It's early yet. We've only just got started."

"Ja!" agreed Petr who only sensed the meaning but was more than happy to continue. Edda was not sure which tack to take. Things could only go downhill from here. She looked at Vera. Vera shrugged philosophically. She knew what Petr was like when he got started but Edda hated to be the cause of it. They were all right for now but if they stayed much longer they would never get George away. Vera decided,

"They no stop drink. You go Novak. They sleep. We see tomorrow." Edda pulled a wry face and nodded in agreement. She was too tired to argue.

"I'll call a taxi," she said to Vera, who came to help her because she knew Edda would not get the address right. When the taxi arrived, George and Petr had disappeared to the bottom of the garden where loud, off-key singing could be heard. She gathered that George was remembering some of his cradle songs.

Back in their guesthouse, Edda and Ofelia crept into the kitchen and made themselves cups of chamomile tea. The Novaks had gone to bed already; for it was gone ten and they would be up before six even on the weekend. Edda was concerned about George's behaviour.

"I don't want him to make a nuisance of himself," she told Ofelia. "I hate to take advantage of my friends. After all we are an added expense as it is, and you know that these people don't earn as much as we do."

"Stop fretting!" Ofelia advised. "Petr and George chose to drink and were having a great time anyway. I'm sure it won't affect your friendship. Cement it more likely."

"I hope Vera takes it that way."

"Of course she will. She's a dear, isn't she? She knows her Petr and if it weren't George on a Friday night then it would be someone else. Right?"

"Yes, you're right Ofelia. I'm being oversensitive as usual." Edda tutted to herself.

"That's part of what's great about you Edda; your sensitivity. You go right to the heart of the matter and you have the courage to act on it. Look at us now. We would not have embarked on the Quest had it not been for you."

"Really? Then I don't want to be the one that is responsible for hurting you, either." Ofelia came over and hugged Edda reassuringly.

"That can be the burden of too much sensitivity," she said. "You go overboard and get out of hand. Listen Edda. I believe you will stand by me through this, no matter what comes. I believe all this was meant to happen. It's destiny."

"There you go again," Edda said. "Making these profound and prophetical statements."

"Yeah!" Ofelia's head swung up to the right, her eyes studying something unseen on the ceiling. "I think you should phone Anthea quite soon."

"I'm going to e-mail everyone tomorrow. We agreed."

"Yes, but . . . I think you should phone her now."

"Oh, for goodness sake Ofelia!" Edda felt exasperated, but she grasped the phone and dialled through to Canada. But there was no reply, because at that moment Anthea was walking up the pathway to let herself in on the night that Dave would be round for that visit. Ofelia was a little ahead of herself on this one!

Early the next morning Ofelia again urged Edda to call.

"But it's one in the morning. She'll be fast asleep!"

"Doesn't matter. Call her." So Edda called and awakened Anthea from her sleep on the sofa, where Dave had left her. She was pleasantly relieved at the animated reception. She realised that her daughter had had an epiphany of sorts. Edda, who had suffered greatly for her daughter, found it difficult to quell the outburst at the tremendous relief she felt. But she dared not ask too many questions. She had to allow Anthea to share in her own time. Edda knew of old, Anthea's resentment should she appear to be prying too closely into her emotional life. She was simply grateful that this Dave, this brother of Ofelia, had managed to break through in some miraculous way. After the phone call, she turned to Ofelia in amazement and asked her if she had set a meeting up for Anthea with her brother.

"Good grief, no!" Ofelia exclaimed with a smile of delight appearing on her face. "I knew, sensed, if you like, that Anthea was closed up tight inside; hurting. And I wanted you to call because she was heavily on my mind. I wasn't sure why. But Dave, no. It would never occur to me to set them up together. I suppose they met to enquire about our progress?"

"I really don't know, but she told me to tell you she had a good conversation with him. I think she likes him." Edda shook her head in wonder. "You are a strange girl sometimes, Ofelia." Edda gave Ofelia a warm hug. "Thank you dear."

"What for?"

"For being you."

"Let's find out how George and Petr are feeling this morning," said Ofelia, "I hope they weren't too awful."

"They probably fell asleep in a heap somewhere and I hope Vera had the sense to leave them. I just hope he'll be fit for our lunch today with Mirek's family."

George's head was pounding. He sat across from a chastened Petr at their kitchen table. Vera was plying them with black coffee and pretending to be cross. George knew from long experience with women that Vera was not as upset as she sounded, but he wished she would shut up. He sighed heavily.

"Enough! Enough!" shouted Petr, still laughing, at his long-suffering wife. Vera subsided and left the room to get on with something else. George delved into his pocket and found a pill. He carried pills for such occasions. This one looked like a Tylenol-Three, a great painkiller prescribed once by his doctor for some injury or other. That should do the trick with a litre or two of water. He wished he could remember what time they were having the meeting with the landlord's family. *Christ! He hoped it wasn't for lunch!* He guessed that Edda would be mad at him, and he couldn't really fault her on that, but he had been having such a good time. Petr did not appear to be suffering as he was. He must be inured to the stuff. *Lucky beggar! Good guy, Petr. He would love his family to come here and meet them all. Why had he not returned to his roots sooner?*

Petr ordered a walk. They sauntered along the streets down to a small park and back again while the analgesic began to work and rehydration set in after all the water he had drunk. When they re-entered Vera's kitchen half an hour later, he almost felt like a new man. She had laid out the table with a typical Czech breakfast. There was dark rye bread slices and small white rolls, cold meats, cream cheese and some fruit. It looked simple and appetising. He found himself feeling good after breakfast and then said he must leave.

"I drive you my car," Petr said.

"No thank you. I walk," George said in the same vein.

"I drive," Petr said.

"I walk," tried George again.

"We drive," Petr said. They drove.

George gave Vera a hug, thanked her in his moderately pigeon Czech and invited them both to dinner quite soon; time to be arranged. Then the two buddies set off for the guesthouse to face the music.

"We're good buddies," said George affectionately to Petr as they drove along.

"Baddies?" Petr eyed George, unsure. His English was severely limited.

"Yes. Probably that too," George said ruefully, and gave Petr a friendly punch on the shoulder. Petr drove complacently onwards. He was a relaxed sort of fellow and was really enjoying the visit with his

Canadian friends. He didn't care two hoots whether anyone thought he drank too much. He only drank in company anyway and anyone could see that George enjoyed a drink.

George figured he could handle Edda's disapproval, but he admitted to himself that he was nervous. Petr insisted on coming in when they arrived. He wanted to say hello to the Novaks. They were friends of his parents and he had arranged the booking in the first place.

"*Ahoy pani Novakovo!*" he called as she opened the door to them. George scurried in and tried to get to his room before the girls caught him. He was lucky enough to get into the bathroom for a shower before they realised he was home. *God! I will have to mind my Ps and Qs or they'll be reporting to my wife*, he thought.

Much refreshed and feeling almost normal, he dressed in clean clothes and descended to brave his friends. They greeted him without a word of reproach.

"You look good, considering!" Ofelia said to him with a smile. "I think you had a good time last night. How do you feel?"

"Pretty good actually," he said, casting a shifty glance in Edda's direction. But she was trying to have a conversation with Petr which was not going too well. George saw an opportunity to redeem himself, as his Czech was lately growing better than Edda's in spite of her year spent living here.

"Let me help," he said politely.

"I'm trying to thank him for his hospitality last night," she said without a hint at the extra hospitality he had extended to George. "And I think I managed that but I'm trying to invite them out for dinner on Sunday and I'm not sure I'm getting through to him."

"Leave it to me," George said magnanimously. "Petr my friend," he said in Czech. Then, "You and Vera free Sunday afternoon?"

"Ano!" said Petr.

"We go restaurant. Eat," continued George in Czech.

"Ano! Dobry!" *Yes! Good!* They smiled at each other in satisfaction and gave each other a hearty slap on the back.

"That was easy," said Edda. "I wish I could do that." George shrugged casually, pleased that he had done something useful.

"No problem!" he said. "When are we meeting with Mirek's lot?" he asked.

"One o'clock at the Prague hotel." George winced slightly.

"Prague?" he said.

"Yes. Hotel Praha. Just off the Square, here in NJ."

"Oh! Good!"

"Fancy place. You'll like it. Not expensive. It's Novy Jichin's claim to fame, from the 'gay nineties' as they once were called, you know? When 'The Waltz', that daring symbol of progress, sent the continent crazy with delight," said Edda with flourish.

"That's great. I'll pay! My treat," said George. Edda turned away. She didn't want an argument but they had agreed to share their expenses equally. George wanted to make amends but Edda was not going to let him get away with paying for his misdemeanours with money.

George began to feel irritated. He could sense Edda's displeasure. *Why shouldn't he treat them to dinner?*

"Edda," he began. She spun round.

"No George! We *share* everything that we do together. We agreed. Now if you feel you have to *pay* to make up for last night, let me tell you are wrong."

"What do you mean?" he asked. Ofelia put her oar in.

"George! You can't pay your way out of this. Anyway you didn't do anything wrong. Why do you feel so guilty? Don't you have the courage of your convictions?"

George was a little stunned by now. He really did not know what they were getting at. He had a habit of guilt by this stage of his life and by nature he wanted to keep people happy. He wanted to be liked. Yes, he would certainly feel better if he could in some way pay for last night for not coming home early with the girls as he felt he should have.

"I'll tell you what I mean," said Edda, as if Ofelia had not spoken. "I mean that if you want to have a drinking session with Petr or anybody and you think it's going to upset me but you do it anyway, then don't feel that you have to pay for it. You can't pay me to let you drink. You are free to do what you like. Just have the courage to make a choice that makes you happy and stick with it. You didn't exactly do anything wrong did you, last night? You are not married to us you know, and your children are not here to watch you. So what's your problem? Eh?"

"I'm sorry. I don't want to let you down."

"Did you let us down?"

"I shouldn't have been so oblivious."

"Then don't be!"

"I'm sorry!"

"There you go again! Apologising! So you had a few drinks in good company last night. Do you regret it?"

"Well no! I think we all had a good time."

"Then why are you saying sorry?" He was no longer sure why he was saying sorry. He chewed his bottom lip and tried not to apologise for apologising. Edda threw her hands in the air with vexation. Petr, who had been watching the exchange with interest, now stepped forward and put his arm around George's shoulder.

"Happy. Happy," he said with a beseeching expression on his face. George was so forlorn and the pair of them were such a comical sight that both Edda and Ofelia had to laugh. George smiled too, and realisation dawned. For him at any rate, Happy Drinking was O.K., but he had to remember that when they were about Quest business, moderation was called for. He felt that he was learning.

Canada

Dave and Anthea sat opposite each other in a booth at the Penny Whistle in Guelph. They had met for a drink. It was a public place so Anthea felt she could cope. Dave said he wanted to show her pictures of Ofelia as a child, when she was known as plain Little Mary. In the dim light Anthea studied the serious little girl. She was smiling into the camera but her eyes held a wistful faraway look.

"She was like that till she was about fourteen and then she suddenly changed. Wow! Emergence of the Teeny Monster." Dave laughed at the memory. "We loved her though, and I think she loved us. We all got on great. But when puberty hit she barely related to our parents. She'd listen to me and Ed and Rich, if it suited her. That's when she changed her name to Ofelia. Rich and Ed and I, we started calling her Feely, then, but she didn't care. She said she was stepping into no-man's land until she could find her true self. Bit dramatic, we thought, but that was the way she became, and has been ever since. I used to think she meant she wanted to find out about her past history but I realised after a year or two and a few deep discussions that she really wanted to find her personality; as her own true self. Do you know what I mean?"

"Yes, I think so," Anthea said. "You wonder anyway, what brings you to a place in this life. You wonder how things lead to events and whether you could have prevented them. Or you wonder if this life is a destiny that you have to live out whether you like it or not." Anthea realised which road she was going down and sharply reined herself in. She quickly said, "I imagine that being deserted as a three-year-old would be devastating, even if you couldn't remember the facts accurately."

"Mmm," Dave mused. She could see he had paid attention to her previous comments and she fervently hoped he would not refer to them. He moved on however. "Feely is a bit psychic, I think," he said. "She comes out with the strangest things sometimes. Take the time, just before she met any of you. She had come round our place with that dick-head of a boyfriend she had. He was telling her they should go on a visit to England; meet his grandparents who still lived somewhere in Kent.

"Huh!" she said to him. "I'm flying right over England. And it won't be with you!" We all looked at her and Ed asked what she meant. She looked a little startled herself, I remember. "I don't exactly know," she told Ian. "But I will be flying to Europe. I'll fly over Paris and over Germany. Maybe I'll land in Russia." She laughed it off then, but by the following week your mother had booked their seats to Prague."

"That's uncanny!"

"That's Ofelia!" Dave smiled at her. "I'm glad you decided to meet with me tonight," he said.

"Well it was to do with our common interest." She was a little defensive.

"I mean I'm glad I didn't totally frighten you off with my persistent tactless personality. I promise I won't bring the subject up again," Dave said, daring thus to mention without actually mentioning the painful subject of her dead child.

"Thank you!" was all she said. She went on to tell him what her mother had written. Comparing e-mails, they discovered nothing new.

"It seems as though they may get somewhere after the meeting with this family of Mom's previous Czech landlord," Anthea said.

"I don't see how they can possibly find anything out," Dave said. "Ofelia knew absolutely zilch about her background; just this assumption that she was middle European from some Slavic country, and no doubt communist at the time."

"Yes, but it was more than coincidence that her shawl had the emblem of the town Mom taught in when she was in the Czech Republic. That was too weird."

"How do you know that the emblem doesn't belong to other towns as well? I mean it's typically middle ages. It could apply to somewhere in Bulgaria, for example," Dave said.

"Yes but don't forget Ofelia's psychic ability," Anthea reminded him with a grin. "This is more than coincidence."

"I do hope you are right." Before Anthea could protest he had ordered in two more drinks. Anthea succumbed. She was enjoying his company and it was a long time, seven years, since she had been out alone on a date with a guy. Even if this was not exactly a date.

They found themselves talking about themselves again. Anthea did not mind telling people about her job. During the week she painted pictures for the illustrations of children's books. She had always liked fantasy and her artwork fitted right in with the popular "fairy" genre of today, so she was kept quite busy and made a fair living at it. She still did the market on Saturday mornings because it was a pleasant contrast to her week and a time where she could mix with other people in a casual, friendly and undemanding way. She needed that.

She told him about her brother Bruno in Afghanistan. His face glowered a bit. Anthea hesitated. "Do you know him?" she asked.

"Not personally!" he stated. "But my wife does!"

"Oh . . ." Anthea was embarrassed.

"Don't worry!" Dave advised. "It was after we had split up." He laughed at her discomfiture. "It must be difficult having a bit of a notorious brother."

Anthea raised her eyebrows and shrugged her shoulders. "Yup!" she said. "Being in Kandahar may give him fresh insight on life. I rather hope it does. What about your brother Richard? How long has he been in England?"

"He's been gone a few years now. He left to visit our Dad's grave and relatives and decided to stay."

Andrea knew that they were both skirting around the subject of her past. She felt that she owed him some kind of an explanation and besides, he had made her feel better. Still, she was reluctant, afraid even, to show gratitude. *He might think she was coming on to him or something.* She really did still have a bad reaction at the thought of the slightest suggestion of intimacy when it came to men. Men were all right as long as they were not connected to her. Any man connected to her was a potential murderer. It was as simple as that.

"I was divorced seven years ago," she said, and went on swiftly to get it over with.

"He spent two years in gaol and then left the country. He probably felt as bad about it as I did. I was and am glad that he disappeared. I don't expect him to *ever* reappear. I just never want to think about it again." She paused and drew a wavering breath. "But of course I do. I think of it again and again. It's a movie that goes round and round in my head until I feel I will blow up." Dave again reached out his hand. Anthea put both of hers out of sight on her lap. "After I told you, actually spoke the words, I felt some kind of release. When I cried it was sorrow. Sorrow for my little baby who died and was not grieved for, because I think I have lived in denial. I couldn't go beyond the horror of him dying. I couldn't forgive . . ." Here she made a valiant effort to control herself. She was good at self-control. She succeeded, and gulping, she said, "Let's walk for a bit." Dave quickly went to pay the bill while Anthea put her coat on. They went outside together and found that a light snow had begun to fall.

Dave tucked her arm through the crook of his elbow.

"Keep us both warm and stop you slipping," he said, sensing that she might object. She did not mind, as it happened. She actually enjoyed the comfort. She felt a tiny crack appear in the hard shell she had built around herself. It was good to be able to walk like this with a nice friendly kind of man and to like him, just a little bit. No strings attached, no commitment, no talk of love or marriage. "I love it when it first begins to snow," he said, looking up into the lamplight at the circling flakes. It's kind of Christmassy." He gave that little laugh of his again.

"I think I prefer May and June, when everything is freshly green again," she answered. She shivered and he pulled her arm a little tighter. "Thank you David," she said. She gave him his full name. He looked down at her.

"For what?"

"For helping me up a very big step."

The Czech Republic

Hotel Praha, The Prague hotel, had been grand in its time but nowadays had a faded air. So far, perhaps, no one had found the necessary cash to bring it back to its former splendour. It stood opposite the gates of the castle of Novy Jicin, right in the centre of town. On a summer's day it was lovely to sit outside with a latte or a beer and watch the small world of Novy Jicin pass by. The castle fountains splashed while small children played and there were often a few tourists taking photographs. But in November, the dinginess was more apparent.

Inside, some attempts had been made. The place was certainly not falling apart, but the beautiful mouldings on the ceiling had been repainted in a sharply contrasting shade of dark salmon against the cold white paintwork. The eye level décor was strictly functional. On the whole, there was a slightly grubby air to the place.

Our three friends entered, casting their eyes about with interest. "I'd love to redecorate this place," Edda said. "Gosh, but it could look beautiful."

"It does look seedy," agreed George, following her gaze. "Wonderful old world structure. I suppose this is a newer building." Ofelia looked at him in disbelief.

"Newer?" she said.

"It can't be more than a hundred and fifty years old. Don't forget, my dear Ofelia, that most of the buildings in the centre of this town are three or four hundred years old and more." Ofelia was silenced. It was hard to keep remembering. Her mother and father's house back in Guelph was only thirty years old and had needed all the windows changed last year and there was a leak developing in the basement. If everything was left, the house would never see fifty years, never mind two or four hundred.

Edda led them round the corner of the L shaped dining room to where she was expecting to meet their guests. There was Mirek, coming towards her and pressing a kiss on each cheek. "*Jak se maš?* How are you?" He was smiling with pleasure.

"Mirek! I am well!" She turned and introduced her friends. Ofelia noticed that Mirek stared at her with interest. They were ushered to their places at the large table, where they were in turn introduced to Mirek's family. Grandad was there and shook Edda's hand heartily. There was Mirek's mother, Erika Dvorakova, looking slightly on edge, and beside her a young woman called Radka, who was also decidedly nervous.

Once seated and armed with drinks, which Mirek insisted upon ordering, they regarded each other expectantly. Where to begin? The alcohol seeped relaxingly into their veins and George, for one, began to feel confident of a promising outcome. Ofelia sipped sparingly. She wanted to be clear headed. She wanted to freeze time. She felt panic rise in her throat like gall. George laid a hand on her arm. "Drink!" he ordered. She drank. He should know. The bitter herbal bite of Becharovka trickled down her throat with welcoming warmth, almost immediately loosening her tension. Erika leant over and put her hand on Ofelia's as it lay on the table. She spoke in Czech and Mirek interpreted.

"Listen, my dear. My husband helped refugees in the 1980s. There were many who were in danger from the government." The young woman, Radka, on her other side stole a nervous glance at the nearby tables as if there could be spies even today, ready to report their subversive chat. Erika turned and patted her arm, obviously trying to reassure her. She continued to speak. "In those days we could trust no one. You had to be careful to whom you spoke, even in your own family. My husband and I took part in what you might call 'partisan' activity. There were very many of us, but sometimes we did not even know who our colleagues were. A slip of the tongue at the wrong moment and the StB, the Secret Police, would be at the house, interrogating. We have seen our neighbours carried away for much less than we were doing."

"What were you doing?" Ofelia asked. Edda gave her an admonishing look.

"Be patient!" she scolded.

"No! It's alright," Erika said to them. "We were a halfway house for political refugees." Here she smiled deprecatingly. "We hid in our house some of the bravest people of our country. Sometimes, these refugees would go from house to house for many weeks until they could safely arrange to be escorted over the border into Austria. Those who did this escorting were the brave ones. I want you first to understand that we had no records of the names of the people we hid. This was the safest policy, you see." Ofelia had to speak again.

"What about children? Were they ever 'escorted' over the border?"

"Only occasionally, when either the mother or the father was seriously involved and they decided to bring their children. Of course, we hated it when children were involved." Erika shivered. "They were so innocent and they always suffered one way or another." Erika fell into a minor reverie; Radka looked as though she might start crying at any moment. No one said a word and into the waiting silence came her next words. "I remember only two such occasions with children," Erika hesitated. There were two babies, twins. The mother had been involved with riots and narrowly missed capture in Brno. She was actually pregnant when she came to us. It was 1981. She lived here and in the neighbouring towns at different addresses for six or seven months before the children were born and old enough to leave. She and her husband left together, each with a baby strapped to their front. Things would have been all right. They often were. But on this particular night, well, they were seen and shot at. The father got away but the mother and the one baby were killed outright. The husband was heartbroken, and of course, blamed himself. He returned to his last address, that's how we eventually found out about it. The StB caught him and God in heaven only knows what they did to him after that. He was sent to Siberia eventually. This information was always given to us at public addresses from the Town Hall steps in the square. This is his daughter, Radka, the remaining twin, who was brought up as an orphan of the state and was reunited with her father only after he was released in 1990. He died last year. These situations affect us in different ways," Erika said, wrapping her arm round the sad looking girl. "Radka does not like to be reminded of her past but she is brave enough to want to help you if she can."

"How can she help us?" Ofelia asked almost tenderly. "What did she know?" Ofelia's eyes reflected Radka's pain. Perhaps she had a great deal in common with this girl.

"She knows that you too are the child of parents of spirit. Men and women who would not stand by and watch their people be betrayed by the rest of the human race." Ofelia experienced a fierce sensation of pride but she noticed the look of shock on Edda's face at these words of Mirek's mother, and saw George who was bred to these ideas take Edda's hand under the table and hold it gently.

"I am sorry, Mrs. Edda." Erika Dvorakova looked genuinely sorry. "But when the rest of the world appears to desert you, how else can you think?" Ofelia had tears streaming unashamedly down her cheeks.

"Was my father really one of these people of spirit?" Ofelia asked.

"We think he must have been," Mirek said. His grandfather nodded sagely and both Edda and Ofelia wept silently into their drinks.

The waitress, who was a young trainee, had been hovering in a worried fashion for quite a while now. She could see no way of interrupting this emotional party and take their order, so she went off to fetch her supervisor who returned with diplomacy and her order book.

Mirek took it upon himself to order for every one. He also ordered a fresh round of drinks and thought to himself. *Thank God for the numbing power of alcohol.* He had not had so much excitement since his mother had bundled him into a manure cart at fifteen and sent him to live for three months on his grandfather's market garden. *God in Heaven! Had he ever stunk!*

"Can you tell us about the second incident with children?" George asked of Erika, when everyone seemed ready to move on.

"Yes!" said Erika. "This was a year or two later. Mother, father and a four-year-old boy came through and successfully made it to Vienna. We heard about it several months later as usual." They went to America and that was the end of them." She sounded dismissive.

"Did you only hear of the ones who came through you?" asked George.

"We heard about many. We always thought we recognised our own. Perhaps we did not pay so much attention to those we did not meet." Ofelia and indeed Edda and George too, looked disappointed.

"Tell us your story, Ofelia," Grandad encouraged. "Let us hear what happened to you." And so Ofelia now took centre stage and told again the story of her early memories. It was exactly the same as Edda remembered, and she could see that Mirek's family was impressed.

Conversation halted with the arrival of the dinner and every one tucked in; even Radka and Ofelia were hungry. Soon, as appetites diminished people's thoughts began to take shape again and need outlet.

"We know other people," Erika began. Radka nodded enthusiastically. "Other people who were involved between '68 and '89."

"There were always people," Mirek said. His grandfather nodded in agreement, eyes shining with the memory.

By the time the meeting drew to a close, Erika had agreed to rally her contacts from those days and see what could be discovered. She felt sure that they would find something. She wrote down the particulars of Ofelia's "suggested" date of birth, 1983, and her probable arrival in Toronto in 1986, which would also have been the year of her escape with her father. Ofelia's hope knew no bounds.

The following day they tried the town hall. From here they were sent to the library to research "historical" information, but they sensed the reluctance, almost to the point of being suspicious and unfriendly. They gave up and walked home.

They hung out hopefully for a response from Mirek's family. It came the following day. There had been a local man called Jan Smutny. If he could be found, he would almost certainly have been involved. The trouble was, Jan Smutny had moved on without a trace many years ago.

"Oh, this is depressing," said Edda. "Where on earth do we begin to find Jan Smutny?"

"It will all fall into place; you'll see," Ofelia announced quietly.

Slovakia

About 200 km away in the small community of Stara Lesna, Slovakia, in the High Tatras, the foothills of the Carpathian Mountains, which run from Poland and along the borders of Slovakia and the Czech Republic, a man sat with his head in his hands. His name was Dalibor. Tomorrow he would travel to the Czech republic to visit his mother, which he did at this time every year. He hated to return to the scenes of his past. They were not good memories. Of late, he had been having a hard time sleeping. Recurring dreams disturbed his nights. Things should have been peaceful for him now, and yet they weren't. He had led a good life, struggling to do his best and acting bravely on his beliefs. Why should doubt and worry begin to cloud his life, now? He did not think it fair. He was sure he had come to terms with his actions during those dangerous years. Why should his peace be disturbed all over again?

Dalibor had been a seriously active dissident in the days before the end of communism. He truly believed that it was he and people like him who had hastened the downfall of the hated regime. He had specialised in helping with the escape of "wanted" parents, who brought their small children also needing to escape. There was always more risk and therefore more dread when children were involved, but Dalibor was believed to have had a strong streak of luck. Certainly his success rate confirmed this, up until that night in '81, while working with his partner Jan Smid and the parents of twin babies. He'd had a bad feeling about it from the start. It wasn't so much that they were barely six months old, but that their mother was still weak. He felt that she had not fully regained her strength. Perhaps too, her attitude was no longer so ruthless. Motherhood had softened her. Dalibor had not been so confident on this job and he feared, even to this day, that somehow, stupid as it may seem, he lost his "luck" that night and a parent and child had died because of it. The father had allowed himself to be caught and his remaining daughter had been taken into care; communist care! They disappeared for many years into the cruel and unnecessary Russian penal system. Both father and daughter were irrevocably impaired by the experience. Because of this, Dalibor had vowed not to deal with parents and children anymore. However, he had in fact continued helping other needy people to escape and even on occasion smoothing the secret entrance of others. It was a game too compelling to give up easily, as long as one did not have to endanger children.

And then came the day, in the summer of 1986, when his own brother, Zdenek, came to him from the far north, in Bohemia. He brought his small daughter, almost three years old. Her name was Michaela, known affectionately as Myshka. In a tragic accident, her mother had been killed leaving father and daughter alone. Dalibor knew that his brother was as involved as he in fighting the communist regime. He had dreaded what his brother was going to say next.

"I want Myshka out of this system and away to people I know of in Canada."

"No Zdenek! Take her to her family. Our mother lives nearby, or your wife's mother lives in Decin. This is the better thing to do." But Zdenek insisted.

"The authorities already suspect me. They watch both our parents' houses. I'm sure of it. You and I know that it was no accident that killed Katya. It was a warning, and if I'm not next then I'm afraid they will contrive to take Myshka away from me. I know you can do it, Dali. I want to go with her. But I will come back when Myshka is in safe hands."

Fool! Idiot that he was, Dalibor had agreed and had set the wheels in motion. Myshka was successfully removed from danger and never seen again. He still could not bear to think of his hopeless efforts to get her back that took a year of his life.

To return to the Czech Republic for the Advent visit was suddenly ominous and depressing.

The Czech Republic

Petr and Vera had chosen the nearby town of Stramberk for their restaurant outing for two reasons. The town would be celebrating its winter festival in the square, a traditional treat for them all, and Petr had friends he wanted the Canadians to meet. Pani Elishka, his mother's friend, had always allowed Petr, as a child, to play with her grown up sons' railway set. You had to push the trains around the track by hand but the intricate landscape plan that her older son, Zdenek had set up years before, kept Petr occupied for hours while his mother and Elishka talked below. He knew that pani Elishka's granddaughter lived somewhere in Canada and he felt that this could be meaningful to his Canadian friends on their quest.

Stramberk stood on a hill topped with a tall and ancient tube of a tower, the town's claim to fame. It lit up the darkening sky as they drove in at dusk. The winding streets of the hill town were entirely unsuitable for cars, so they parked in the lower part and climbed up through the steep, narrow streets to the square. They had reserved seats at the Shipka Hotel, and were not due there for another hour. This would give them time to explore the Christmas market.

The square was always set up for market by November. It was filled with little wooden huts, each one a unique store with enticing wares. Each also had their glowing brazier to keep its occupant warm and send a further shaft of heat towards the customers. If that were not enough, there were plenty of vendors with hot punch steaming and calling to be sampled.

"Mmm! Hot mead," George said, but Petr urged him on because he wanted to introduce his friends first.

Street musicians were playing Christmas melodies, adding to the cheerful atmosphere. Down between the rows of huts they went, Petr barely allowing them time to pause and admire. George and Edda protested when a stall devoted entirely to cookie cutters insisted on their attention. The cutters were small medium and large, and in as many different shapes as was imaginable. Christmas trees, angels and stars were just the beginning. There was a dachshund cutter that caught Ofelia's eye and she joined them in their search.

"Look!" said George, keen as any girl. He loved making cookies and the cutters reminded him of the set his mother had used. He'd never seen them in anyone else's Canadian home. *Whatever happened to those old cutters of maminka's? Oh look! There was a pony kicking his heels and there was a rooster. And that cat. How Carly would get a kick out of that.* He bought some at once, including a complete set of farmyard animals with a large goose cutter and three matching goslings.

"Come quickly!" Petr urged. "I have someone for you to meet." Ready now, they gave him their full attention and followed him contentedly through the milling crowd. Not far on, Petr stopped at an open stall where an older man was doing a fine trade in hot mead.

"*Dalku!*" he called to him in the vernacular. "*Ahoy!*" The man looked up and a huge smile lit his face at the sight of Vera and Petr.

"*Petru! Verko!*" he called. Ofelia was electrified. The very tone and inflection of his voice sent a shiver down her spine. She reeled and clutched Edda's arm as her head spun. She stared at him. He was surely simply another Czech guy whom they were about to meet. Petr introduced him as a good friend of his family.

"My good friend Dalibor!" he said. Dalibor shook each of their hands. When he came to Ofelia he hesitated ever so slightly. Perhaps it was simply her dazed expression. The moment passed and soon Dalibor was smiling genially again and handing them each a small glass of the hot, sweet honey wine. He drew to their attention, the woman behind the counter selling cookies.

"My mother, Elishka."

"Ahoy pani Elishko!" Petr beckoned them together.

The woman leaned forward to shake all their hands. "Elishka," she introduced herself. She realised they were not Czech and immediately asked where they hailed from.

"*Kanada!*" Petr said proudly.

"Ah so!" said Elishka, casting a glance in her son's direction.

"Where in Canada?" he asked.

"Guelph. It's in Ontario," George said. Of course no one had ever heard of Guelph. They chatted for a while, sipping the warming mead, exchanging casual information about Edda and her friends' visit to the Czech Republic.

"I have come to find my roots," Ofelia stated. Dalibor, and even Vera and Petr looked a little puzzled.

"She means she is looking for her family," said Edda. Dalibor nodded politely, a small frown still creasing his forehead.

"So you are Czech?" he enquired of her.

"Well, I think so . . . I hope so." He nodded then went on to explain his own visit from Slovakia, where he lived and taught skiing, and organised hiking in the summer.

"Every year I come to help my mother at the Christmas market in November," he said. "Christmas markets are a long tradition among Czech people and not even the many years of oppression have prevented them from continuing," he explained. "My mother and I have made our own tradition by sharing this together." He put an affectionate arm around her as he spoke. But she whispered something urgently. His face expressed reluctance. She nudged him. "My mother wishes you to know that she has a granddaughter, my niece, my brother's child, in Toronto."

All eyes darted towards her with interest. Dali continued with mild embarrassment, "She wishes to know if you might know of her." George saved the day.

"I am originally from Slovakia and have friends in the Czechoslovakian community in Toronto. Perhaps someone there knows her. What is her name?" A look of sheer pain crossed Dalibor's face and he made to speak, but Elishka was too quick for him.

"Michaela Velkovskova," she said eagerly.

"Mother! Mother please!" The distress was clear. "Thank you George, but you must understand that we no longer have contact with her. Many children were taken to the safety of Canada during the years of communism. They were officially adopted by Canadian families. She will no doubt have another name now and will not be connected with the Czechoslovakian community. She could be living anywhere in Canada."

"You don't even know what her name became?" George asked, almost scandalised, completely forgetting the fact that Ofelia didn't know her birth name either.

"Sadly, no," Dalibor said. Ofelia began to chew her little fingernail. *Were there more people in Canada just like herself with no knowledge of their roots?*

"So you have no connection with her at all?" Edda's brain was whirling .... *Could this be ... ?*

"None!" he said curtly.

They were caught up in a sudden realisation of the vastness of the human dilemma, their own quest but a drop in the ocean of reality of lost souls. The subject was dropped like a stone though Ofelia wanted very much to talk, but she was sensitive to the pain Dalibor emanated. The distress was palpable on all sides. Even Petr and Vera, upon whom the interchange had been partially lost, knew something painful had happened, and had Petr been at all aware of Dalibor's activities during the eighties he might have been able to shed more light on the subject, but as a child of those bygone days, he had been told nothing that could endanger him or the people involved. He knew nothing of Dalibor's dissidence.

As for Dalibor, the meeting had indeed disturbed him greatly and further added to his general feeling of discontent. He turned to greet and serve some new customers. At the same time, Petr suggested that they should be heading for the hotel and hurried goodbyes were said before there was any resolve on their disturbing conversation. However, it was uppermost in all their minds as they sat with an aperitif at the bar at the Shipka.

"Petr! What did Dalibor do during the eighties? Was he a 'dissident'?" asked George. But Petr was not able to understand. Ofelia broke in and said,

"He had to have been involved to a certain extent, because of his niece. You could see how upset he became when we talked about it?"

"Really?" said George and Petr echoed him.

"Tsha!" Vera looked disgusted with them. "They see nothing. Men!"

"I usually do." George said, offended at Vera's tone. "I did notice that he became sad for a while and I thought of my own three girls and how lucky I was and probably unappreciative in my case. My parents escaped from Slovakia during the war, don't forget. It might have been before I was born, but I still heard the stories. It must have been unbearable for some of the people here. We can have no idea."

"Maybe we do," came Ofelia's small voice. "I feel like the torn off bit that was sent to safety." This sentence was lost on Vera and Petr. What did come out of their discussion however was that they would telephone Dalibor and ask if they could talk tomorrow and tell him of their own quest. This made Ofelia feel better.

Back once more at Vera's house, Petr looked up pani Elishka's number and called straight away. There was an excited back and forth conversation between Petr and whoever was on the other end. Eventually Petr put his hand over the mouthpiece and said to them, "Dalibor go." He ended the call and spoke rapidly to Vera, who translated. They listened avidly, chipping in where necessary for clarification.

"Dalibor no stay here. He go Slovensko now."

"You mean he's left already? Why Slovensko?"

"He live in Slovensko."

"In *Slovenia?*"

"No Slovenja! Slovensko."

"Oh right! You mean *Slovakia*. Why did he leave so suddenly?"

"I not know," Vera said, and gave an eloquent shrug. Apparently Dalibor had cut his weekend short and left almost immediately. Elishka was pretty upset about it. They looked at each other thoughtfully.

"What do you think?" Edda asked Ofelia.

"I think," she said slowly, "that we should try to find out a bit about him. Perhaps his mother would be able to help us. She might know whether he was involved and could put us in touch with other people who were too. After all, what do we expect of him? All we know is he lost a niece in Canada..." Ofelia had an air of fragile vulnerability about her. They talked about it some more and it was decided that Vera would call the mother and have a little "chat".

The call, however, was not entirely successful. Although Elishka admitted that she had, to her sorrow, lost her three-year-old, only grandchild in 1986, and that she had been sent to the safety of Canada, she had no idea how that had been achieved. They would have to ask Dalibor, but she was afraid that he would not know much more about it than she did. Vera also learned that Elishka seemed almost afraid to talk about it. It was as if she had not yet thrown off the fear of bygone days.

Slovakia

Dalibor, for of course this was he, had driven away from his mother's house in Stramberk in a state of anger and confusion. He stopped at a small hotel in a town beyond the Slovak border and booked himself a room. Then he went down to the bar and got drunk. When the barman refused to serve him any more, he went up to his room and fell asleep sprawled upon his bed without even removing his shoes. He woke at five in the morning. Out of habit, he dragged himself to the bathroom where he downed half a litre of water and had a good hot shower. You could always rely upon the water being hot at this early hour of the morning. Dalibor returned to his bed after drinking another big glassful of water and fell back to sleep for another three hours.

He was on the road again by nine, feeling a lot better physically but still not satisfied in his mind. Those Canadians. They had stirred up his already painful memories. He felt impelled by forces beyond himself to try once more to find his niece. But he had no idea how or where to begin.

Snow began to fall as he drove higher into the mountains. Soon there was quite a blizzard. If he drove slowly he stood a chance of making it home in time for lunch. Home was only two hours away in good weather. He turned on the radio to try and hear the weather forecast, but the reception was terrible, much worse than usual. Conditions worsened and he could see no sign of the next village, which he should have been through by now. He wanted to wait there until the weather improved.

He rounded a bend and saw, almost too late, a car skewed across the road ahead. He ill advisedly applied his brakes at the unexpectedness of the apparition and although he had been driving at a snail's pace, he skidded and came to rest parallel with the little car, luckily not touching it. His passenger door prevented the other driver's door from opening. He hopped out and ran round to find a young man. He was English or North American, and seemed grateful that Dalibor could understand him. He said that he had swerved, taking the bend too quickly. By trying to emerge out of the snowdrift, he had only managed to place himself dangerously in the middle of the road. There had been no traffic for quite a while now, he was thankful.

"Only a fool would be out in this," Dalibor laughed ruefully. "We are two fools I think."

"We sure are," the young man agreed. "My name's Rob Halley. I'm from Canada, and I teach English at a business school in Krumlov." They shook hands.

"Dalibor Velkovsky. It's a pleasure." They both laughed at that. And something small and urgent flashed at the back of Rob's mind. He wanted to give it some attention but there was no time. The temperature was dropping fast and they had to hurry. They could not stay where they were. With two of them on the scene they were able to push their cars around. They decided to put Rob's smaller and highly unsuitable car to the side out of harm's way, and take Dalibor's four-wheel drive to see how far they could get. Dali felt that they were extremely close to the next village but the falling snow made it impossible to get their bearings. They decided to press onwards to find civilisation.

Canada

Meanwhile, Cleo had been doing some much-needed research. She knew Edda and Ann well enough and although she did not know Ofelia as yet, she could tell that she was a dreamer. And Cleo was always ready to help a true dreamer. The moment the trio left for Europe, Cleo had begun her investigation. First, she went to see Ofelia's adoptive parents. Over a friendly chat and a cup of tea, she found out what she wanted to know. Backed with credentials and a letter from Ofelia's parents, the Kingsleys, Cleo made an appointment with social services in Toronto. But this time, with a little charm, she managed to dig a little deeper. She had been shown a short descriptive sheet recording the recovery in the park of a small child, reported by an unknown caller, and including a bad photograph that bore little resemblance to the Ofelia of today.

"Do you work with adoption agencies at all?" Cleo asked of the woman before her, innocently, after she had explained her interest in Mary Morton's adoption.

"Not if we can help it. We do not want children who are likely to have been bought or sold," said the woman testily. "After all, agencies usually deal with children from overseas whereas we have enough of our own children to find parents for. Of course, these agencies occasionally have a case that they don't know what to do with, like the case of Mary Morton." The woman nodded carelessly at the pitifully thin file that summed up the contents of Mary Morton's arrival into the system.

"How do you mean?" Cleo asked.

"Well," she began, "she must have come in through an agency that was set up to help overseas refugee children. In those days there were lots of escapees from European communist countries. Mary was obviously from Europe, but she had no documents, but then I suppose they didn't dare to leave any identification on her." Cleo drew a slow breath and held it carefully. The woman continued, "Of course we always thoroughly check to find out where children like this come from, but in this case we obviously found nothing. Mary *had* to be accepted by us in order to be helped." The woman sighed. "What else could we have done? She was pretty sick, it says here. It was mighty irresponsible if you ask me." A small silence ensued while Cleo pondered upon the lack of interest of the young woman before her.

"So it's possible that an adoption agency had received Mary Morton illegally and then put her in the park to be picked up because they were afraid she would otherwise die?" pursued Cleo.

"Well, I dare say that was what happened. But I can't really say. It was a long time ago and we have a whole new set of refugees now, illegal or otherwise. That's where our attention is focused now." The woman tucked a stray wisp of hair behind an ear and surreptitiously glanced at her watch. Cleo persevered.

"Is there perhaps an older person I could talk to, with a little more experience?" Cleo stared her out and was pleased to observe a flush appearing on the woman's face.

"Just a moment!" she snapped and disappeared. It was over ten minutes before someone returned.

"I'm so sorry to have kept you waiting." A pleasant and friendly woman in her mid-forties came forward with an outstretched hand. "I'm Beth Smythe," she smiled. "I think I may be able to help you." Cleo looked at her hopefully, and when Beth suggested that they go for lunch, she willingly agreed. "I'd like to talk and find out a little more from you about Mary Morton," Beth said as they walked out of the huge building to a small restaurant in the vicinity, and over a tasty hot fish curry, Cleo told Beth briefly about her own connection with Ofelia's search for her roots in the Czech Republic, and how she had been found wandering sick in a park near Morton Street at the age of three in 1986.

"I want to see if I can help them from this end," she explained. Beth's eyes gleamed.

"I don't want to raise your hopes," she ventured. "But there is something I want to straighten out to satisfy my own curiosity as much as yours." Cleo tensed with expectation. "Let me tell you a story about a mouse," Beth began with a smile. "It was May, I think, in 1988. A man had come from Czechoslovakia, searching for his niece. He called her Myshka, or mouse in his language. The department wanted to help him as much as they could, so they palmed him off on to me. I was a junior employee at the time, keen, and willing to do a little research. I made the phone calls for him because his English was unpractised and he would never have managed on his own. The enquiries led to the child who had been lost in the park: Mary Morton. We examined her file, but even when I showed him her photograph he said that it couldn't possibly be her."

"Why couldn't it?"

"Well, apart from the fact that he didn't recognise her, he had received a letter saying she had been adopted by a family in Toronto, so he did not believe that she had been found in a park. Especially as . . ." Beth frowned and hesitated.

"What?"

"You see, little Mary was thought to be mentally impaired." At this Cleo gasped.

"Ofelia certainly isn't that," she said.

"But she certainly was very sick when she was found and photographed. She couldn't or wouldn't speak."

"Yes," murmured Cleo, "That's probably why they left her to wander in the park. They couldn't cope with her. After all, they couldn't call a doctor and setting her out in a park like that was probably the only way they could help her."

"Mmm . . . And it was an understandable mistake on our part too, thinking she was impaired. I suppose those who deserted her in the park would have to assume that we had had her fostered or adopted and then perhaps they wrote to inform the family in Europe. Except that the man from Czechoslovakia had received no specific information."

"Do you think the Czech man was mistaken about Mary Morton's identity?" Cleo asked. "Are you thinking that he really could have been her uncle after all?"

"I don't know. It would have been understandable if her uncle failed to recognise her in her condition. But there's a bit more," Beth said. "You'll have to come back to the office with me. I've got something I want to show you." Cleo hastened to gather her things. They paid and left.

Back in the office Beth disappeared for quite a while, leaving Cleo waiting impatiently. When Beth came back she was holding something with excitement. "I have here a copy of a birth certificate that was mysteriously submitted in 1989. This may or may not be connected with Mary Morton." The two women stared at each other. It was one of those moments when time was pinioned and the possibilities spilled over. "I'm afraid to raise your hopes." The fragile piece of paper in her hand trembled between them. "But look at this." Beth spread the birth certificate on the desk between them. "*Michaela*,' She read. '*born*,' (I suppose that means,) '*seventh of something 1983.*' Now this must be her mother and father; '*Katerina Velkovskova and Zdenek Velkovsky*'. Funny how the mother's and father's names are not exactly the same, eh?"

"Mmm," Cleo agreed absently, her mind fixed on more immediate information. Something didn't gel. "This date ties in with Ofelia's age. So there's a possibility this girl may be her. When did you connect Mary Morton and Michaela . . . er, Velkovskova?" Cleo leaned over the certificate and read the name haltingly. Beth laughed.

"Just before lunch actually! The officer who asked me to help you jogged my memory." A light went off in Cleo's head with a bang.

"Oh! What was the uncle's name?"

"His name was Dalibor Velkovsky." In the stunned silence several questions jostled simultaneously in Cleo's head. Beth helped her out. "I had been transferred to Ottawa for training for three months in 1989. By the time I returned to Toronto in early 1990, I was immersed in my career. The time spent with Dalibor Velkovsky in 1988 looking for

Michaela was hardly uppermost in my mind. Also, there had never been a birth certificate in our files in the name of Velkovsky until this one here," she said, indicating the document on the desk between them. "Then, about four years ago, while I was checking out a South American child, also with the initial 'V', the Velkovsky birth certificate came up and hit me right between the eyes. It had been filed in 1989, all on its own with absolutely nothing to connect it to anything except the place where it had been mailed from, somewhere in central Toronto."

"What did you do?"

"Well for a start, as I told you, I've only just thought of it. And anyway, what could I do? I had lost touch with the uncle. This piece of paper only points to the fact that Michaela Velkovskova was connected to our department, however tenuously. I suspect that somewhere in my brain I still connected Mary Morton with Michaela in spite of Mr. Velkovsky refuting it, but until today, with your arrival, it never clicked. And even if it had, what could be gained by upsetting the adult Mary Morton with the mere hypothesis that she might be this other girl?" Cleo stared at her. Something did not feel quite right.

"But now, don't you feel you owe it to her to tell her who she might be?"

"But my department doesn't really know if she *is* Michaela Velkovskova." Cleo stared uncomprehendingly. They had just looked at her birth certificate. Or so it seemed. Surely there was a connection. "You don't get it, do you?" Beth asked. "We have this information *on file*. You and I have just come to a shaky conclusion, but the ball lies in your court. It is not our policy or responsibility to tell you who we think you are! But if ever you, or anyone connected wants to follow up, the information is here." Beth rapped the edge of her hand meaningfully on the desk and Cleo smiled slowly as the realisation dawned. *It was Ofelia's quest, not Beth Smythe's of Children's Aid . . . but given the way events turned out today . . .*

"So, if we can track down this uncle . . . . Gosh Beth! If I hadn't met *you!*"

"But you *did*."

"Thank you so much Beth Smythe. And please thank that woman who first spoke to me," she grinned.

"A moment like this is what makes the job worthwhile," said Beth tremulously.

"I can't wait to pass this news on," Cleo said. "This is absolutely wonderful." Beth put up a warning finger. "Be careful. Let her know it is only a clue. Nevertheless I think it is an exciting clue, if they can find the Velkovsky family, and I wish her every success with her quest. She is lucky to have such friends." And with that, Cleo was soon winging her way back to Guelph with two copies of the birth certificate firmly in her possession.

Cleo got home at four o'clock that afternoon. It was nearly five by the time she had reported to Ofelia's adoptive parents, who reported it to their sons, especially Dave, who telephoned Anthea right away. And Anthea had just heard from Cleo as well. There was great excitement and everyone went straight round to Cleo's address where she said she would telephone the Czech Republic as soon as they were all gathered.

The Czech Republic

It was just after eleven p.m. when the phone rang shrilly in the little guesthouse in Novy Jicin where they had, of course, all gone to bed. Mr. Novak answered the phone, supporting his loose old pyjamas with one hand. His wife hovered anxiously behind him. He hollered down the phone, but obviously the people on the other end hadn't a clue what he was saying.

Cleo said,

"Edda please, or George or Ofelia." Well! Mr. Novak understood that all right, but had no need to call them because all three were huddled at the top of the stairs, peering down in the dark. They had a good idea that the call was for them. They just could not think why. Edda took charge. She spoke to Cleo who said that she had been doing a bit of research and that she would like to talk to Ofelia. And would she make sure that Ofelia had paper and pencil handy. Edda handed the phone to Ofelia.

"It's Cleo. For you! She has some information." Then she hurried to get the paper and pen. Seconds later when she returned she saw that Ofelia had gone into a kind of trance.

"I don't believe this!" Ofelia kept repeating in a hollow whisper. She looked vacantly at Edda who tried to give her the pen. George grabbed the phone.

"Hi Cleo! It's George. Ofelia is sitting down before she falls down. I don't know what you've told her but I've got a pen in my hand. Do we have to write something down?" He began to write as Cleo dictated. "I've got it!" he said. "Anything else? O.K. I'll pass you back to Ofelia." Ofelia listened carefully as Cleo again went over the results of her visit with Beth Smythe. As the name Michaela and Velkovsky reverberated in her ears, her head spun and a choking sensation in her throat prevented her from speaking coherently,

"We...we met the Velkovskys today. Uncle and grandmother...Oh!" She looked wildly at Edda, who waited wide-eyed for an explanation. George, who knew what was happening, was still staring tensely at the notes he had taken down.

"Ofelia! Ofelia!" Cleo shouted ineffectually down the phone from Canada; from another time, another place.

Edda took up the phone and listened while Cleo repeated the details yet again to make sure they got their story straight. "Look! There's no real proof that Mary Morton and Michaela are one and the same. It is a lead that could well be a dead end for the Velkovskys too," Cleo urged. She was herself in shock. How could such coincidences be? And what if she had not taken it upon herself to go that extra mile on behalf of her friend? Thank God she had done it. Pulling herself together she agreed to send them copies of Michaela's birth certificate if Edda would arrange a fax number for her.

Cleo then insisted that Edda briefly explain how they had met the Velkovskys. Was it really Dalibor Velkovsky and his mother? Cleo also asked, incidentally, if George was behaving himself. Edda laughed and said he really was and then they rang off.

None of them could get to sleep after that. They had to sit up and talk about it. George came into the girls' room bringing his supply of Slivovitz. Edda refused but produced her own bottle of Becherovka, the herbal liqueur that she had bought to counteract George's apparent necessity of throwing back Slivovitz. Becherovka, a mild, herbal liqueur made from the healing waters of the great spa of Carlovy Vary, must be sipped! She had decided to buy some for moments of stress or celebration and they could not be sure which this was going to be. The news was startling. It was uncanny, even frightening, especially for Ofelia. Zdenek and Katerina Velkovsky, as stated on the birth certificate; who were they? Did any of them dare believe that Little Mary Morton was Michaela Velkovskova? Only Ofelia was certain of the connection and nothing the others said would move her from this. She kept rocking gently and repeating, "I know it. I know it."

Edda and George decided they would have to phone Dalibor again first thing tomorrow. They must get in touch, even if they had to go to Slovakia and the High Tatras to find him. Ofelia decreed it was as if they had an angel on the trail with them. They did not laugh when she said this. It was too close to the truth.

That night, Ofelia dreamt that she was looking down into a dark pit from the depths of which a man gazed sadly upwards. She called and called to him but he could neither see her face nor hear her voice.

The following day, at last, had a sense of real purpose. But as Ofelia was restless and George, wondering silently if the "good times" were about to end, seemed disconnected, Edda took charge with renewed energy. Her practical side was in a state of disbelief. *This was melodrama bordering on surrealism. This was taking serendipity into the realm of the ridiculous.*

"This seems too ridiculous!" cried Ofelia on cue. Edda had to smile.

"Quite melodramatic, eh?"

"God yes! It's almost surreal! But there's no such thing as coincidence, Edda. You know that's true."

Edda stared briefly and with no little wonder at Ofelia, then set about phoning Vera to bring her up to date. She copied a fax number from Vera's office where Cleo might send the birth certificate. Vera was excited and promptly arranged a few days off work, leaving Sharka to receive the fax. Vera phoned Mrs. Velkovskova to announce the upcoming arrival of her three friends with interesting news, and drove to the guesthouse to pick them up. By noon they were all headed for Stramberk.

Elishka Velkovskova was waiting at her door, curiosity personified.

"You have news from Canada?" She was overwhelmed with curiosity. Nobody was willing to mention Ofelia's part in the enquiry yet and Mrs. Velkovskova had so far failed to make any connection. Vera was in charge of translation, and rough as it often was, she made a grand job of it.

A friend in Canada, she explained, had been to the authorities and discovered the birth certificate of Michaela Velkovskova from back in the late eighties. A copy was being sent by fax to Vera's office.

"But where is Michaela?" said the wide-eyed Grandmother. "Did they find my little Myshka too?"

There it was again, Myshka. Ofelia could hear her Tati's voice as clearly as a bell. But everyone was too busy tending to the older woman to notice Ofelia's agitation.

"We must call Dalibor," encouraged Vera. The call was made but there was no reply. Dalibor could not yet have arrived home. His mother left a message indicating that she had incredible news.

"He always calls to tell me when he arrives home," said his mother. "Then I know he is safe."

Following this, a call from the office confirmed the arrival of the faxed birth certificate.

"Fax is here!" Vera said. "What we do?"

"Ask Sharka to read out the details on the birth certificate," George said. Vera repeated what Sharka read.

"Father is Zdenek Velkovsky.

Mother, Katerina Velkovskova.

Daughter, Michaela. Born seven August 1983."

This was certainly the birth certificate of Dalibor's niece and Elishka's granddaughter.

Oh God in Heaven. Elishka sat down paling visibly. Kindly, George sat beside her and took her hand.

"But what does it mean?" she said tremulously, "Where is Michaela?"

"Here . . . Here I am." Ofelia's dramatic whisper answered the question.

At that point Vera, who was still listening to Sharka on the telephone, cut across.

"Sharka also have fax story. I go fetch." The eyes in the room turned bemusedly from Ofelia towards Vera and watched her race out of the door. Edda rushed to calm Ofelia who was close to tears.

"No Ofelia, no. You mustn't raise Elishka's hopes until we are sure. Yes, it is definitely her grandaughter's's birth certificate, but we must wait a little . . ." Edda exchanged a look with George who had been trying to answer Elishka's host of incomprehensible questions to no avail.

They had to wait for Vera's return, so Elishka brewed a much needed pot of coffee, a ruse to occupy her hands as much as to serve her guests. With Vera's return, the birth certificate was passed around with great interest. Edda read aloud the brief account Cleo had made of her time with Beth Smythe and Vera translated the salient bits. Edda asked for paper and pencil and Vera did the same so that they could make all the points in two languages. This kept them busy for a while during which

Ofelia and Elishka glanced surreptitiously at each other. After half an hour and several arguments a list had been compiled by Edda and Vera with Ofelia's and George's help.

1986
1. Small, sick girl, wrapped in a shawl, found wandering in a Toronto park with no papers.
2. She is given the name of Mary Morton because she will not speak.
3. A family in Guelph eventually adopts her.
4. She keeps her memories to herself, but she can remember a word or two of Czech, which she thinks must be Polish.
5. Her old shawl bears the ensign of Novy Jicin, which is the town Edda has taught English in. She thus realises that she must be Czech. (Possibly from Novy Jicin)
6. Further enquiries by Cleo lead to the discovery of a birth certificate handed in anonymously.
    a) Could belong to the child who was found in the park and taken in by the Canadian authorities.
    b) Was definitely connected to the Velkovsky family in Stramberk.

"And according to Cleo," said Edda, "The woman she spoke to in Toronto felt that there *might* be a connection between the birth certificate and Mary Morton." The gap was closing but they needed additional proof. There was no call yet from Dalibor. Then George asked if Ofelia had shown the shawl to Elishka.

"Oh no!" she said. "I didn't think." She unravelled the shawl from around her neck and handed it over. The very instant her old eyes fell on it Elishka emitted a keening cry. She half stood, her hand reaching out towards Ofelia, her voice a broken appeal.

"Myshka? Our little mouse?"

Ofelia was in her arms in an instant.

Dread followed joy in quick sequence in Edda's emotions. This couldn't be happening.

After a long moment Elishka sat down on the sofa, her Michaela close beside her. She said,

"This shawl was my last gift to you. This shawl, my own mother wove for me. I gave it to you, full of love to keep you warm on your terrible journey. You *are* Michaela Velkovskova. And look." She turned a corner of the shawl and showed them a small, embroidered "M".

"This I sewed myself. This is astounding. I had never dared hope for this day." She sank crying into her chair, overwhelmed by tears. Somehow, nothing was lost in Vera's translation of Elishka's words. The room was electrified. Feelings of amazement, powerful and overwhelming, swirled. Ofelia, (or was it Michaela?) studied the embroidered "M", as if she'd never really seen it before.

George wiped the drips from the end of his long nose with his sleeve and suddenly became all business. Sniffing, he said,

"We have got to find Dalibor." Instantly they agreed but continued hugging each other at least one more time. The joy in the room struggled to overcome Edda's fears. *This was wonderful news, but Ofelia's father? What of him?* She could see Ofelia out of the corner of her eye repeating the name, "Mich-a-eyla Vel-kovs-kova, Mich-a-eyla Vel-kovs-kova."

And so the day wore on. They were all on tenterhooks. Petr joined them at three, after work, but there was still no news from Dali.

To pass the time, Elishka told them about the time when her daughter-in-law was *murdered*, as she put it, by their government.

"I was alone, of course," she said, adopting a martyred tone. My husband was in prison while my oldest son Zdenek and his young wife Katya and baby Michaela here, lived in a village far away to the north near Decin in Bohemia, so I did not have the comfort of seeing them very often." She smiled brokenly at her granddaughter, who was still seated very close to her. She squeezed her hand.

"Why was your husband in prison?" Ofelia wanted to know. Elishka answered in the tone of one who thought that would be obvious.

"Because he refused to join the communist party. We were used to such things but the worst part of it was that our sons were not allowed to go to university because of it, and they were both very clever boys." She paused to wipe a tear from her eye with a small cotton handkerchief. "Then the authorities, I should say their spies, found out that Zdenek was involved in anti-government activities. This was a crime that, if proven, they punished most severely. They did not of course require much proof. In this case a threat was issued to Zdenek by way of a warning. He was imprisoned locally for three months during which time he lost his job. There was nothing his company could do to help him. They had to obey or their company would suffer. You could not expect a company to go down for one man." Elishka's face became embittered. "Of course my son, he would not stop, would he? Even though he had a wife and baby,—and a mother." Here there was a long pause while she regained her composure. "Next thing, Katya is walking to do her shopping and a car runs into her and in an instant, she is dead." Ofelia's hand went to her mouth on an indrawn breath at Vera's harsh translation of her mother's death. Elishka turned towards her, crestfallen, "*je mi lito*. I am so sorry!" But she continued perforce, "The police never found the perpetrators of this murder. They killed my daughter-in-law and left my grandaughter motherless." Elishka and Ofelia were crying openly and of course there were tears in the eyes of all present. "And this act of mindless cruelty was to teach my unteachable son a lesson." There was no scrap of doubt in Ofelia's mind that she had found her family. This was her mother that they were talking about and a cold grip had hold of her heart.

"When can we go to Stara Lesna?" she said. Everyone stared at her. "I want to find Dalibor as soon as possible," she said.

"Yes!" agreed Elishka when this was translated for her. "I too will come." This was a statement, not a request. "But first I tell you what happened next. Everyone turned to her expectantly. This was a compelling story. They wanted to hear more.

Elishka continued, with Vera's help and often a large dictionary.

"Now I expected that Zdenek would bring this grandchild to me or to Katka's parents, but no! He was afraid for her life. He believed that it was little Myshka that they would now seek to destroy." She wiped her eyes and sniffed. And so Dali, my other stupid, blind son agreed to help him take her out of the country. Oh so wrong for a child who cannot make her own choices." Edda could bear it no longer and went to put her arm around the distraught woman.

"You needn't say any more. Please don't distress yourself so. This is a horrible memory for you." Ofelia was sitting, white as a sheet, just staring. George looked grim.

"I shall finish my story now that it is begun. My little Myshka got safely out of Czechoslovakia with her Tati. She was secretly smuggled into Canada and given to some foreign people as their child. No more was she a Czech girl. Her history was gone. She was too young to remember anything. She was scarcely three years old when she left. If her father had stayed with her she would have had a father to keep her connected with us, but instead he came back and was taken and sent to jail in Russia. I never saw him again. I do not know whether he is alive or dead." Her lip was trembling." It is a terrible thing for a mother to lose her children. And now Dalibor, my second son, seems also to be lost. What kind of a world is this?

There was nothing anyone felt like saying. George thought about how his parents had escaped probably in much the same way to Austria where they had lived before immigrating to Canada. For that matter, how on earth had his father managed to fight with the Brits during the war? Neither his father nor mother had ever discussed their experience except in the merest detail. Now it was too late to ask them. Realisation of their experience flooded over him in waves.

Edda was troubled that they had found the family all right, but where was the father? Where was the uncle? Edda did not want a tragic ending, especially after all the raised hopes.

But Ofelia said, "Whatever happens now, I think every moment will have been worth it." Then she turned and spoke directly to Elishka, slowly so that Vera would understand and translate very accurately.

"Mrs. Velkovskova. I believe you are my grandmother. *Babichka*." She faltered. "And if I am wrong about this, then I would still like to be your adopted grandaughter." Tears ran down her face and Edda found herself now rushing to comfort Ofelia.

"Oh my dear!" Elishka said, reaching out her hands. How sad if you cannot remember your mother and father."

"But, you see, I *do* remember my father. He was with me but then he went away and I only remember great unhappiness and confusion."

Elishka Velkovskova looked at her grandaughter thoughtfully. What great miracle was this? Was it possible that it was only half a miracle with the other half still to come? Could Zdenek be returned to them too?

It was three days before they were to receive news of Dalibor. The weather had turned cold, and early winter storms had been reported in the mountains. By the third day, they were really worried. Elishka put a call through to an emergency number in her son's village. A neighbour told her that Dali had not yet returned but had not been expected until today, and anyway the roads had been impassable because of a bad winter storm. The weather and the roads were clear now and he would be sure to tell Dali to phone as soon as he returned. Was there a problem?

"Was there a *problem?*" Elishka cried. "My son left Stramberk already three days ago. He may be lost in a snowdrift on that abominable mountain where he so foolishly insists upon living. Yes! There *is* a problem. Please report him missing in Slovakia and we will do the same here."

Panic ensued. They were informed that search parties were already out all over the Carpathian Mountains looking for careless travellers who had managed to be caught in this unpredictable weather. An extremely frustrated Home Rescue force worker who had been out without rest for three days reportedly asked, *"Will they never learn?"* However, they added the name of Dalibor Velkovsky to their list and the make and registration number of his car, which of course, Elishka had been unable to remember and they had needed to look up. This apparently caused further frustration and it was an hour later that the phone rang with a message from the wilds of the High Tatra mountains. Dalibor's car and also a small Hyundai had been found by the wayside within two kilometres of each other. The Hyundai was a rental car from Ceske Budejovice, and they had the man's name that had rented it, Robert Halley. The other car was Dalibor's. Neither car had occupants. The cars had been marked with a notice pinned to the windshield. Authorities believed that the two men could have teamed up and tried to walk because Mr. Velkovsky's car was only a short distance from the nearest hamlet, just half a kilometre. Of course, in that weather half a kilometre would seem like forever and the visibility must have been nil. However, the weather was very clear now and they were assured that every effort was being made; helicopters, search parties, and dogs. They would soon be found.

And in the minds of the anxious recipients of this news, further words rang fearfully in their ears. *Dead or alive!*

There was no time to waste. They must pack and leave for the mountain town of Zilina where they could receive first hand information as soon as it came available. Petr would drive Elishka in her car with Vera, while George, Edda and Ofelia were to follow in Petr's relatively new Skoda. They left after lunch and by four o'clock were well over the border into Slovakia heading east and climbing all the while.

George was driving and enjoying the scenery. He decided that he really must write a long letter to Ann about the adventure and its effects upon him. This was the country that his parents had fled so many years ago. It all seemed so distant in more ways than were obvious. Would life ever be the same again? He wished he could spend a couple of days seeking out his relatives in Bratislava at the end of Ofelia's (or was it Michaela's) quest before joining Ann and the girls for a visit in France and before heading back to Canada. He guessed he'd have to return one day soon. He knew from experience that it would in fact be easy to sink back into the old complacency. But he had never before realised the effort and courage it took to leave the country of your heart to save your family from oppression, to give them a new life of freedom in an alien country, as his parents had done. He knew more than ever how precious Ann and his girls were to him and he prayed to his unfamiliar God that when he returned, he could find a way to make a meaningful difference in their relationship.

His prayers were interrupted by Ofelia from the front seat, saying, "Look, the others are stopping. Good! I need a break." They had entered the town of Zilina. Edda pulled herself out of a doze as they drew into a small square and found a parking spot alongside Petr's car near a little restaurant. The sky was very clear and blue up in these mountains, and the temperature was icy. The cold hit them as they walked to the entrance. Inside, the atmosphere was warm and welcoming. Their host came forward smilingly to offer them a table near the glowing hearth. With slightly better appetite they ate a light meal. Ofelia and her newly found grandmother sat together exchanging occasional smiles. They were both still pale, mostly on account of the tension they were feeling about Dali.

Vera, their spokeswoman with the authorities, phoned for an update but received none. She announced their presence in the town and left her mobile phone number. Then, on the restaurateur's recommendation they went to book in at the hotel called *U Slunce*, The Sun, on the other side of the square. Later, still without news, they met for a drink in the bar and a walk before bed. All they wanted was news of Dalibor. Good news!

Slovakia

When Dalibor and Robert had tried to continue driving to the nearby village, within ten minutes the snow had become impassable. Dalibor knew they were in a mortally dangerous situation. Neither he nor Rob were dressed for the extremity of the weather. Dali cursed himself for his stupidity. If he had not been so wrapped up in his unsolvable past he would have checked the weather, or at least looked up at the sky. He had been living too long in the mountains to have any excuse. He had one sleeping bag in the back of his car and a rather thin old blanket. They would have to do.

"We've got to get out of the car and find a more sheltered area," he told his companion. "The car will freeze and I don't have any candles which might otherwise have helped for a while."

"I've got matches," Robert volunteered.

"Bring them," Dali said and reached in the back to gather the blanket and sleeping bag. "We'll make for those trees." Dali pointed off to the right. They left the car unlocked and struggled in the direction he had pointed. They kept falling into drifts and the going was slow but once in among the trees it became easier. Then the trees thickened and the undergrowth of brambles and holly became rampant. In the eerie silence the only sounds were their gasping breaths and the crackling of branches as they hacked their way through, keeping to deer paths where they could. Suddenly the thicket ended and to their immense surprise, they emerged into a dense part of the forest where no snow had penetrated. The tall trees formed an awning that covered the sky with their faraway tops and held the snow from the ground beneath their feet. The atmosphere was charged with energy. It inspired great awe. The air was warmer here and they were also heated from their struggle through the undergrowth. They smiled hopefully at each other and looked around for a good spot to make camp.

"See through there!" Robert said. "That looks like a clearing." They moved forwards to find signs of life: some bales of hay lay scattered about.

"What's this?" Robert was surprised.

"Huntsmen leave hay for the deer," Dali explained. "Keeps them alive and well fed for the hunt." He laughed.

"Very funny!" Rob said.

"It is true," Dali said. "Huntsmen look after their prey. It makes good sense. And after all, they love their deer." Robert shook his head in wonderment and gratitude to the hunters as he gathered some of the hay for their bedding. They were obviously here for the night.

Dali showed Rob how to gather up extra hay to put over their blanket for later. Meanwhile they gathered sticks and wood. With Robert's matches, they soon had a warm fire going.

The two men settled and watched the flames. They had no food but a bar of chocolate and a couple of bottles of water. They would survive for a while. They were not worried. They felt strangely contented and united in rapport, companionable in their hallowed clearing with the firelight flickering on their faces.

Rob told Dali that he came from a small town in western Ontario called St Helens. He had been drawn to the Czech Republic since boyhood, when he had heard of the Velvet Revolution of the Czech people in 1989. And although he said nothing to Dali, he remembered vividly that day in the Old St Helens Store when his mother and neighbour Dora had discussed the little girl who had lost her name. He had written her name down, hidden it in one of his books for safekeeping and forgotten it. Now he could not still a persistent nagging at the back of his mind.

What was her name?

Dali related stories of his days in the rebellious years and of the loss of his brother and niece. It eased his mind to talk about it, and for Rob, it reinforced an eerie sense of deja vu.

Gradually they fell asleep on their hay mattresses, after piling more hay over themselves for added insulation. The fire died down to a glow as the men slept long and dreamlessly. The forest creatures came shyly out to eat the hay on the other side of the fire. One little deer stood cheekily eating hay right off their beds.

On the third day, Dalibor Velkovsky and Robert Halley walked blithely from their haven, found Dali's car as he had left it and saw the time check pinned on it by the police. They drove to fetch Robert's car and then back to the village that they had originally been seeking, blissfully unaware of the consternation they had caused and also of the fact that they had slept for over thirty hours. Nobody believed their oblivion. People thought they had got their days mixed up. Neither man had the words to argue, as both had sensed something beyond their worldly understanding and neither had hitherto believed in magic.

Dali had wanted to leave for Stara Lesna and home straight away, and having exchanged e-mail addresses had said his farewells to Robert. The police however wanted Dalibor to return with them to Zilina where there were people waiting to see him.

"What people?" he said explosively.

"Your mother and several friends from Czech and Canada." Dali was silenced. Again he did not argue. *The Canadians?* He thought.

"Good!" Robert said. "That's my direction too. Our acquaintance will be prolonged. Great!" The chief of police added that Dali could leave his car here if he wished, as he could certainly be escorted to Zilina and back if he wanted.

"Let me drive you," Robert invited. I have to return my rental car soon, so I must drive back that way." He felt a great urge to meet these Canadians too.

"Fine!" Dali accepted. He hoped there would be no more delays.

Robert followed the police car. On arrival at the police station in Zilina, Dali was surprised at the fervour with which his mother flung herself into his arms.

"Matka, please! I am fine, as you can see," he said, disengaging from her tight embrace. Stepping back, he flung his arms open wide to indicate just how fine he was. His mother threw herself back into his arms again and Dali looked over her head at the little knot of people staring at him.

"What is it? What has happened?" he said, a feeling of fear rushing up his spine. The girl he knew as Ofelia stepped out of the tangle as his mother let go and turned, taking the girl's hand, and bringing her forward towards Dali.

"Our Myshka!" was all Elishka was able to say.

Robert watched spellbound. During his night in the woods, Robert had learned of Dalibor's partisan activities during communist occupation. He had heard Dali's yearning and regret when he talked of his lost niece and brother. There was unfinished business here, Robert guessed, and he had the feeling that things were going to unravel in a totally unexpected way. Yes, it had all begun in the wood, a mystical place; a place of miracles. And now, right before Rob's eyes, a miracle was unfolding. He gazed at the lovely young woman looking up at Dali. At this moment her soul shone from her eyes. He could see quite plainly that they were replicas of Dali's eyes, and instinctively he knew that she was Dali's lost niece.

He waited to see what would happen. Dali took both her hands in his. Turning them over so that he could see the insides of her wrists, he ran his finger up to the crook of her left elbow. Elishka too, peered closely. There, Robert too saw what they were looking for. It was a red birthmark, quite small and also quite faint after all these years, but none the less clearly discernable. Dalibor looked at her face and smiled.

"You really are Michaela, aren't you?"

"Michaela?" Robert whispered dazedly. *Of course! Michaela! The name on the birth certificate. Michaela Velkovskova. Velkovsky . . . Dalibor Velkovsky,*

Dali glanced fleetingly at Robert, sensing his shock. Michaela seemed to sway as she looked at him.

Robert had lived with the sadness of this girl's lost identity since he had been nine years old, and now that she was rediscovered, he never wanted to see her world shattered again. This was the stuff of dreams. Robert's soul took flight.

Even the group of involved police and rescue workers watching the little tableau were entranced.

A whip round was organised and one of them went out and got several bottles of beer and the inevitable Slivovitz. They toasted the re-united family amid tears and laughter and soon an air of gaiety took over which eventually carried everyone but the family and Robert down to the nearest pub.

Ofelia was beside herself and seemed only able to say,

"I can't believe this is happening."

But at last, decisions had to be made about the immediate future. What to do and where to go. Dali had given up all thought of returning to his mountain village and intended to take time off to get to know his niece. But there was something he had to do first.

"Michaela," he said to her. "Let us go and talk together for a while. Perhaps we have a few questions to ask each other."

"Many questions," she said and they excused themselves from the main party and went off to talk. Robert, who was afraid of losing sight of Michaela, and loath to leave the company of his new friends, now needed an opportunity to tell of his connection; surely they would never believe it! He asked, that if they were staying up, if he might join them for a while. They were happy to have him in their midst.

"You will be curious about your father." Dalibor began as soon as he and Michaela had moved off.

"Yes!" said Ofelia, who was trying to think of herself as Michaela. "I have a clear, clear impression of him." Her eyes became faraway, dredging up wisps of deeply hidden memory. *The rough wool of his jacket as he ran through trees, holding me to his chest, my arms and legs wrapped tightly around him, clinging on for dear life.* "I remember his voice: protective, soft, comforting. I also remember that he disappeared one day and did not return." She paused reliving the pain. "I was sick for a long time after that and I would neither eat nor talk. This is why no one discovered that I was from Czechoslovakia."

They had found a bench in a small park and were sitting, half turned towards each other. Ofelia studied the man before her; her father's brother. He was perhaps in his mid fifties, fit and healthy and even tanned from the winter sun. *Would her father look like this too?* Dalibor's voice brought her back to earth.

"I do not know where your father is now. You realise that?"

"Yes I know. Your mother, my grandmother, told us the story before we realised who I was. He is not dead?" She bit her lip.

"I do not know. I tried to find out what happened to the political prisoners after the fall of communism. The ones who were kept in Czech prisons were immediately released but those who had been sent to Russia, the so-called dangerous ones, were not." He held her hand comfortingly as he spoke. "Eventually a list of released prisoners was issued, but I never found your father's name on a list anywhere. I had to assume that he was dead along with many others who had been in this category. He was *known* and that was his downfall. Had he stayed in Canada he would have been safe, and how was anyone to know that the Czech people would be free in 1989? How I wish my brother could have been there to see that day." They were silent for a while. A bitter fear rose up in Ofelia that she would never, after all, see her father, but something within her burst upward and rejected such a loss.

"Tell me, what is the name by which you have been called all these years?"

"I was named Mary Morton after a street near the park where I was found. I took the name of my new family when I was adopted, Mary Kingsley. I never really liked Mary for myself, and when I was fourteen I changed it to Ofelia, from *Hamlet*. You know; Shakespeare."

"Yes, I know it. Ofelia is a sad name for you."

"I was a sad girl. I knew that I had lost something but as I grew up, I did not exactly know what it *was* that I had lost."

"How do you feel about the name Michaela? You do not remember it?"

"No! I remember the word 'Myshka!' That is all. But Michaela feels right. Myshka feels right. Perhaps my friends in Canada will continue to call me Ofelia even though I am no longer sad, but here, and to you, I am Michaela. That is me." She pronounced it the Czech way: *Mich-a-ey-la*.

"I am glad!" he said. "But there is something that I want you to know." She looked up, interested. "I too want to find out more about what happened to your father Zdenek," he said. "Both for you, myself and my mother."

"How can we do that?" she cried. "I want to help!" Dali smiled at her fervour. He could hardly believe this miracle was happening. If only his brother were here.

"What I think we have to do, is find out who was with him in prison in Russia. That should be easier than before because people are more and more willing to talk about their experiences. After our Revolution and the subsequent release of political prisoners, many of us did not know how to deal with our pain. We did not have any experience of how the rest of the world would care. We were reluctant even to discuss it among ourselves. I was like that myself." But she was impatient.

"Where do we start?" she asked.

"Leave it to me to make some enquiries," he said. "Now tell me. How much longer do you have before you must return to Toronto?"

"I will stay as long as I have to. Forever if necessary."

"You have family on both sides of the Atlantic. Your Canadian parents must also be important to you?"

"Oh! They are and I love them. But I must get to know you and my grandmother and find out more about my mother. I have no memory of her. But above all I want to find my father. That was my first reason for coming here."

"Slowly! Slowly! I am very happy that you are here." He smiled softly. "We shall work together on this. Do not worry. But I want you to understand. If we find out that your father is dead, then remember that I am here, and I will be as a father to you."

"Thank you!" she said and put her hand back in his. He lifted it to his lips and kissed it gently with a smile.

Dali said to her,

"Let me tell you about what happened to me when I was lost in the snow."

Ofelia knew that they had been in the woods for two nights but that both men denied this fact, claiming it was only one night. She prepared to listen carefully. He reminded her of their first meeting.

"I met you in Stramberk and we spoke in the market, you remember? You and my brother had been on my mind lately. My memories had become unbearable. I wanted to run from them. I left town that very night."

"I do remember," Ofelia said. "I felt my own loss of family very strongly on that day too." He nodded.

"I drove through the Czech countryside into Slovakia and stopped at an inn to drown my sorrows, as you say." He gave her an apologetic look and she grinned at him. "The next day, Monday, I set off for home and into a snow storm."

He told her about his meeting on the road with Robert and how they had eventually had to leave the car and seek shelter in the woods. He told of their struggle and eventual breakthrough to the calm interior of the forest.

"I cannot explain to you this feeling. We had come from a place of great risk and danger into peace and safety. It was like a great cathedral, mystical and yet magical too. And it was warm, so warm after the snow. In the very heart of this space was a clearance of trees where the forest animals came to eat. Kind woodsmen had brought hay and there was plenty for us to use as bedding with the blankets we had carried from the car. Rob, my new friend, had matches. We lit a fire and were very comfortable. We sat and talked until we became sleepy and the fire died down. We fell asleep and woke with the dawn to see shy forest creatures eating the food left there for them. They observed us but did not run away. We watched until they left then prepared to leave ourselves. We both felt extremely well, although all we had eaten was a bar of chocolate and a little water. As we emerged from the forest we saw that the sun was up and the sky was blue. The road had already been ploughed and a notice had been pinned to my car with a time and date on it. They would be looking for us. The snow around the car was well trampled and there were signs of search going on right in the woods where we had sheltered. Rob said that they had obviously not found us yet! And we were glad that they had not disturbed the peace of our haven."

"They couldn't find it because they were not meant to," Ofelia said enigmatically. Dali accepted this and continued.

"We drove into the village just five minutes down the road and there we discovered, as you know, that we had been missing for two nights and it was not Tuesday, as Rob and I insisted it should be, but Wednesday."

"You slept through a whole extra day." Ofelia did not say this with surprise but with simple acceptance. Her eyes shone. "And then you found me," she said joyously.

"Then we found you."

And the thought came to him that if this seam of luck held then maybe they would find Zdenek. He was very afraid that his brother was dead. Perhaps that was why he had avoided seeking too deeply after

Zdenek's name had not been on the lists of released prisoners. Breaking into his thoughts his newly found niece surprised him yet again with her apparent perspicacity. Could she read minds?

"And we *will* find my father," she announced. "When you were around the fire with Robert, did you talk about me?"

"Yes!" he said.

"And Zdenek?"

"Yes!" he said.

"You see?" she asked, as if it were quite obvious. She had more surprises.

"And if Robert talked about stuff that is important to his happiness, then he too will find what he wants." She gave a small precise nod to confirm. Dalibor did not contradict her, but asked.

"What is this '*stuff*?'" Ofelia laughed and said,

"Oh, it's just a Canadianism. It means 'things' or 'information'."

"It is time we joined the others," he said, taking charge with great delight. It was lovely to have such a charming young niece. "We must all make new plans I think?"

They returned to their friends and found them in a state of renewed excitement. During the absence of Dalibor and Ofelia, Robert had inferred to the rest of the party that he had a story to tell them with direct connection to Michaela's history. Now he began to share it with them all. He took them back to his tenth year, to the day of Dora Andrasky's visit and the overlooked birth certificate; the birth certificate which she had discovered belatedly amidst the leaves of one of her husband Ladya's books and which he had wanted her to dispose of; that same birth certificate which belonged to a little girl who had been left to be taken to hospital from a Toronto park when she was three, a few years previously. Robert related how he had carefully written the girl's name and place of birth and hidden it safely in one of his own books before the decision was made that his mother would mail the birth certificate to the appropriate authority in Toronto. Especially, he conveyed his feelings at the time for that little girl's loss of identity.

When Robert's story had been told, Ofelia went to Robert, speechlessly, putting her arms around him, having no words to express the enormous implications of his actions. Robert hugged her back and felt his loneliness evaporate. Over her head he looked into Dalibor's eyes and no words were needed there either.

No day could ever have ended more perfectly!

Decisions were quickly made. Everyone wanted to return to Novy Jicin and Stramberk, even Robert. He could not abide separation from this company of people with whom he felt such complete affinity. He felt as if his life were just beginning. He realised too, that perhaps Dora would like to know of the reunion of that birth certificate with its owner after all these years. He must contact his mother at the earliest opportunity.

The Czech Republic

The journey back to Stramberk was one of hope. They gathered at the Velkovsky household to make plans.

Ofelia would stay with her new grandmother while Dalibor began the search for clues to Zdenek's whereabouts. Edda would spend a few relaxing days with Vera and Petr and renew acquaintance with other of her friends. She also wanted to be close by to make sure that all was well with Ofelia (or actually Michaela), and that she was quite confident to stay alone. Edda's only consolation in going home at this juncture was that she was to be the bearer of good news. She did not want to leave.

George was to be the first to go. He was flying from Prague on Monday to spend ten days or so in France. His experience had been tremendous and cathartic. He felt released as though he too had been imprisoned all his years. *A different kind of imprisonment than Zdenek's perhaps, but nonetheless,* he thought, *a closing down of the senses, a defence mechanism which can happen when one is torn cruelly away from one's culture.* Of course in George's case, it was his parents who had done all the experiencing, but he still felt that somehow, in his mother's over protectiveness, it had rubbed off on him. Now he was free to move forward in life.

Nobody could tell if finding Zdenek would be quickly achieved. At Robert's suggestion, Dalibor began by tracing his old friend and colleague, Jan Smid. Mirek's family had been unable to locate their Jan Smutny, but they thought that Dalibor might have better luck. Dalibor doubted Jan Smutny's involvement with the twin babies he had tried to help in the early eighties. He was wondering if Smutney was in fact his friend and collaborator, Jan Smid. Dalibor and Robert drove out together searching for a certain village in the Beskydy Hills not far away. There were many obscure little communities dotted around, not often visited by the rest of the world other than by summer hikers but Dali could not for the life of him remember the name of the place, because in those days it had been their constant policy never to speak of personal information. The less known the better.

Robert, who declared himself to be at their disposal for some days yet, eventually suggested getting out in one of the villages and asking some questions. Robert's clear vision was invaluable to Dalibor because without it he seemed unable to make sensible and simple decisions. Dalibor's own sights were clouded by fear and sudden lack of confidence.

They stopped at a little inn and ordered beer. Their host was a man of about sixty. Robert nudged Dalibor.

"There's your man," he said. "He'd have known everything that was going on here." They took stools at the bar and it was easy to start up a conversation because the man was glad to have new faces to talk to in such a sleepy spot. They talked generally at first and the bar man warmed to them. Robert broached the subject first in his halting Czech.

"My friend here," he said, nodding at Dali, "helped with the escape of people over the border to Austria during the days of communism." The man leaned over and repeated what he thought Robert had meant to say. Dalibor helped him understand but lightly brushed off his part in past activities. This he felt was the correct approach. The barman, whose name was Stanislav, rose to this immediately and shook Dalibor's hand in recognition of his bravery.

"There were a few from these parts who did the same thing. They live quiet lives now." That was true enough. There would never be open recognition. Dali went straight to the point and said,

"I used to work with a man from round here called Jan Smid." Stanislav roared with laughter, startling them both.

"Yes! They were all called Jan Smid. But," he continued seriously, "there were two men that I remember talking about in those days. Neither was Jan Smid by name but either of them could be your man."

Dali was disappointed and a little shocked. He had trusted Jan like a brother and yet perhaps he had not even known his real name. But Robert was excited.

"We would like to meet with them," he said and was surprised at the change that came over Stanislav's face.

"You think I would lead you to these men? Never." It was Rob's turn to be shocked.

"Oh, but we would never . . ." He was halted from further words by Dalibor touching his arm lightly.

"My name's Dalibor Velkovsky. *My* Jan Smid would probably remember me and my niece who went to Canada." Dalibor rapidly moved to the next subject. "Stanlislav, we will be staying round here for a few days, doing a bit of hiking. Can you recommend a place to stay?"

"Sure," he said. "Right here." And he called to his wife to show the gentlemen a couple of rooms. The rooms were adequate. Stanislav's wife offered them a fine lunch, which they were ready to enjoy. After that, true to their word they went off on a hike and did not return for several hours. After supper they sat drinking and chatting about nothing in particular to the locals who dropped in. Nobody approached them and it was as if nothing had ever been said. Rob was becoming impatient.

"Don't worry!" Dali said. "We must act as if we do not care. We must be casual. These 'locals', are probably looking very carefully at us. The word will have got around. You'll see."

True enough, after they went up to sleep, a note was pushed under Dali's door. He came straight to Rob's room to show it to him.

"Here! Listen to this." And he translated. "It says, 'Explain the mouse.'"

"What?" Rob didn't get it.

"He means Myshka, Michaela."

"He does? And so . . . . ?"

"There is more. It says, 'Leave the answer on the back of this piece of paper with the landlord. Also write brother's name."

"Whose brother's name?"

"There is only one brother this could mean for me and that is Zdenek, Michaela's father. O.K. Now I will write these things—this stuff!" And he wrote that Michaela was the mouse and her father, his brother, was called Zdenek Velkovsky. Rob then went straight downstairs and gave the note to Stanislav who was chatting to some fellows still in the bar. They all stared at him and he stared back. It was a bit cloak and dagger, he thought, and it felt a bit unnecessary for the twenty first century. But there was nonetheless a current of excitement and he was interested to see the outcome.

The next morning brought a new note under the door. This one read:

Middle of Square ten o'clock.

"This is ridiculous!" Robert said scornfully. But even so, Dali could see that he was enjoying it.

"They need a little excitement, perhaps," Dalibor said. "We will give them some." He said, "Let's go fifteen minutes early and walk around the square. They will see us and perhaps we will also be able to see them, watching us." The two men grinned at each other.

When they arrived in the square it was almost deserted. They casually crossed from one corner to the other in a diagonal line. At a café they saw a group of men and women having morning coffee, but they were completely ignored. They then walked under the old arcade along the side of the square, making a figure seven. Looking down the alley way they saw no one.

They continued along the next side of the square making a right angled triangle and it was then that they saw him; a young gypsy fellow, lurking in the shadows of a shop door, the thick walls around the doorway providing lots of cover.

"There's someone!" Robert said in a stage whisper. But Dali, back in his old part again, was looking the other way. The gypsy darted out and like a snake disappeared several doors further along. Robert was all set to follow but Dali held him back.

"Wait!" he hissed, and sure enough, from behind them, they saw two men creeping back the way they had come. They were not looking because they thought the gypsy had been a good enough decoy.

"What's the game?" Robert said, watching the gypsy out of the corner of his eye. He was making no more moves at the moment but was watching him furtively.

"That's exactly what it is!" said Dali with tremendous satisfaction. The difference being, we won't be for the chopping block when we're finished."

"Good grief!" Robert said with awe. "This sure ain't like Canada."

Dali was not stopping for a discussion. He strode out into the middle of the square. Upon reaching the fountain in the center he realised that there was a man standing on the far side just out of sight. He rounded the fountain and the man came towards him, arms outstretched in welcome. A wide grin split his face.

"Dalibor Velkovsky!" he roared. The men clasped each other in an embrace. Robert watched with awe as these two men who had been through the fires of hell together, met after more than twenty years. Robert found that there were tears in his eyes.

Dalibor drew Robert along and with an arm around each of the men they made their way wordlessly towards the café. Once there, Dali ordered three Slivovitzes which they downed immediately and promptly ordered another round. They laughed at the game they had just played out there in the street, both parties testing each other out following the old rules.

"I knew who we were dealing with the moment I saw the gypsy boy in the doorway. Same old tactics. Who was he, by the way, and how did he know what to do? He is too young to remember."

"Just a young friend wanting to play along," said Jan. "There is a group of interested people who still like to hear the stories of how we coped."

Then came the talk of the old days and gradually it drew round to today. Dalibor told Jan about the unexpected appearance of Michaela. Robert was silent throughout but entirely fascinated. At last Dalibor said, "I was dumbfounded to learn that you were not really Jan Smid. But I can only think of you as Jan."

"You know why it was, my friend. It was safer that way. You may be pleased to know that my name really is Jan even though my surname is Smutny."

"Quite inappropriate!" said Dalibor. "Robert, you know that Smutny means 'sad'?"

"Yes," Robert said.

"Jan was never a sad man."

"You did not have an alias, Dali?" Robert asked curiously.

"No! I never considered it. I don't know why. Perhaps it was because I never believed I would be so deeply and lengthily involved."

"About your brother, Dalibor," Jan's deep voice cut in. "I suppose you realise that he certainly had a few aliases and the papers to go with them."

"Not exactly," Dalibor answered with a frown.

"When he was taken away to prison, his papers named him Tomas Havlik." Dalibor took several seconds for this to sink in.

"But I thought he wasn't released from prison in Russia. We were told that he did not exist when we tried to check on Zdenek Velkovsky." The colour drained from Dalibor's face. "Oh my God!" he said. "So he was released under another name. But why did he not come to us?"

"No, Dalibor, he was *not* released under another name. But he did *escape under* that name. This much we knew and we also know that he got out of Russia safely."

"But, why did we not hear of this?" Dalibor had a break in his voice. "We loved him. We needed to know he was safe. Why did we not hear?" Dalibor pounded his fist on the table, causing several customers to look their way.

"There is a story here, and I will tell it to you very soon, but not here. We must find somewhere more congenial; more comfortable."

Dalibor could hardly wait. He was terrified about what he was going to hear and doubly terrified about what he was going to have to tell Michaela.

Jan had known about Zdenek Velkovsky, alias Tomas Havlik for several years. He knew he was living in Michalovce, in Slovakia. When he took the Canadian, Robert Halley, and Dalibor back to his log house on the edge of the village, he was heartsore to think of the pain the people of his country still suffered generation after generation because of wars and invasions by other nations. He remembered the devastation of spirit and soul of the people. Yet they rallied and still pursued their lives. Even the horror of the Holocaust was taken in hand by those who emerged from it, the Jewish Nation struggling on in the world. Today the scourge continued with the mindless sacrifice of human beings in terrorist attacks, and in society's ever-increasing violence. Jan had often seriously wondered what motivated the human race. He thought of Zdenek's helplessness to overcome his self-recrimination. The State had really done a good job of distorting his mind. Jan was terribly afraid that it was too late for Zdenek to return to his family.

As Jan thought about the best way to break the story of Zdenek's condition to Dalibor, he went into his kitchen to put on a pot of coffee. He got out from his cupboard a large loaf of tough black rye bread and some butter and home cured ham. He believed in the comfort of food. Dalibor was, on his part, relieved to see the coffee and sustenance; he was sick of alcohol and needed a break from it. Besides, he wanted to be clear-headed to hear about his brother. Soon they were settled around the big table in Jan's kitchen where an old iron cook stove delivered a warm glow. Jan served silently. The clock ticked ominously on the wall and at last Dali could stand it no more.

"Tell me, Jan, for God's sake!"

And so Jan told the tale.

Zdenek's Story

The story of Zdenek Velkovsky was a sad one. He had been condemned to hard labour in Siberia, but had managed to escape with two other inmates during an exchange of weaker prisoners for stronger, newer men. Weaker meant, of course, that they were no longer fit for hard labour and were taken by train to a depot near Moscow where they were more or less forgotten for years on end. In a moment of confusion on the train journey, a huge flock of migrating birds blocked the track causing a delay of a mere ten minutes. Three men, all chained together, had rolled off the train and hidden quite easily behind some bushes in the ditch. One of the three had not wished to go, and set up a screaming which was drowned below the shrieking rising birds. However, in order to escape undetected, they had to put a stop to his racket. They knocked him senseless with a nearby rock.

This added to their troubles, of course, because although the forced escapee was no great weight, none of them were, they had no real strength for carrying him either. They waited in the freezing ditch for him to come round and prayed that the guards did not do a head count after the halt. Luck must have been with them, for not only did the man rapidly regain consciousness, but he seemed co-operative, or perhaps, simply resigned. They managed to creep away and make good speed for a couple of kilometres. Fear gave them wings. A boy found them resting on the edge of a small copse and summoned his father, who bundled the men into a cart and brought them to his smallholding in a nearby village where their chains were hacked off and buried in the vegetable garden. The men were hurriedly fed soup and bread and once more in the cart under a blanket they found themselves on the road again.

In this manner they were wordlessly passed from village to village until they were eventually handed a rough hand drawn map and pointed in the direction of The Ukraine. By now, their clothes had been patched, washed or added to en-route so that they no longer resembled prisoners. They were on their way southwest. They had been given an address to memorise in Belgorod, some miles inside the Ukraine. Here they were to seek more help.

The journey to the border took over a month. They often helped out on the small farms along the way, in exchange for food and beds in the haylofts. It was warm and dry and at least as luxurious as their prison accommodation had been. Their physical appearance vastly improved.

The border guards in rural Russia rarely experienced encounters with strangers, and although they were expected to examine papers and generally put the fear of God or communistic vengeance into the locals, they were lax enough to let Zdenek through in his guise of uncle returning his young nephews to their family in the small hamlet just over the Russian border. There was friendly exchange on both sides. The boys showed their documents and Zdenek indicated that he would remain on the Russian side if the guards preferred. As he had been told to expect, the guards just ushered him through with a show of kindness, and never even asked for Zdenek's papers. An hour later the guard had already long forgotten about him and went off duty, which meant that the new guard taking over knew nothing about it. The following day, the same trick did not work for the second escapee, so he returned to the village. After a few days, another "old trick" was resorted to with success: he went through lashed to the underside of a hay wagon.

The third one elected to stay in Mother Russia and may be there still, passing in a vagrant fashion from farm to farm.

The long trek through the Ukraine passed in similar way, but at a more leisurely pace. It was three months and well into summer before Zdenek and his companion, who was headed for Hungary, parted ways near the Czechoslovakian border. Zdenek was nearly home.

He had regained health and strength during the months of fresh air, reasonable exercise and good farm fare but now that he found himself alone, his mind flew back to his deserted daughter. After the hard years of prison life, reality set in. He became depressed and therefore careless, which almost led to his being caught again.

He was camping out at nights. And although people on the whole were anti-communist and therefore sympathetic and friendly to his cause, this was never to be presumed. On the day that he planned to enter his own country he stopped at a farm, knocked on the door, and offered himself for a day's work in exchange for food. The officious looking young man who answered the door immediately asked to see his credentials.

"I have none," Zdenek said.

"Then get out!" The man said viciously. Zdenek did not hesitate. He did not want to get on the wrong side of anyone after this much freedom. He left immediately, taking off across the fields and losing himself as fast as possible.

He vowed to stop no more until he was on his own soil, contaminated as it still was with the hated regime. He lay low near the border watching carefully. He saw his chance after a six-hour watch. A hay wagon was approaching from the Czechoslovakian side. It was dusk and the twilight lent an aura of eeriness to the evening. He waited till the occupants of the cart were well past the guard and a little way along the road, then he approached carefully.

"Ahoy!" he said. "Hello!" They recognised a fellow countryman and greeted him quietly. He joined them as they trundled along and offered them a brief explanation of his situation. They were willing to help in any way to thwart the system but they gasped at the temerity of his plan. They would be returning across the border after they had delivered the hay to the barn that existed some way into Ukraine territory. Zdenek knew that it was often the case that the small country farms criss-crossed the actual borders of a country often by a matter of metres, a fact that had caused no real concern for previous generations. Now that visual borders had been put in with the precision seen fit by the government, farmers regularly had to go back and forth like this. The border guards and the inhabitants alike were unconcerned so long as they knew each other and that too, was often the case. The formality of papers was again often dispensed with. After all, the borders between two countries that were part of one country, namely the USSR, were hardly in need of guarding. Zdenek suggested that they simply wait for the expected change of guard, and drive through as if he had been with them all along. This was the kind of nerve that was needed. But these simple farmers were not practised in the daring work of the partisans, even though they supported it whole-heartedly. However, they were willing to give the plan a try. One of the men produced a jar of some lethal local brew that sometimes was necessary for a little payment at the border, thinking that they could put it to good use now.

One hour later, our friends, having drunk only one, or maybe two shots of the rough liquor, embarked on their return journey with a little more gusto than usual. Starting to sing rather loudly an old and familiar drinking song as they came within two hundred metres of the pass point, they cleverly and politely simmered down by the time they had reached one hundred meters. At fifty meters they stopped altogether as the new guard came out to observe them. They waved in a friendly fashion and continued on their approach.

"Ahoy, Comrades. What have we here?"

"Jaroslav's birthday! But his wife does not want him drunk!" said the older man. Jaroslav sat happily between his brother and Zdenek, with a smirk of delight on his face, which attracted all the attention. He hiccupped for good measure and all present guffawed in pleasure.

"Wish him a happy birthday, my friend," shouted the brother to the guard with a cheeky grin.

"How can we?" said one of the guards with wit. "We must toast him with Slivovitz or our good wishes will lack strength."

"Here! Take! Take!" said the companion, first offering another drink to Zdenek and Jaroslav with more daring than Zdenek thought necessary. The companion took another slug himself and gave the bottle to the guards. Jaroslav protested avidly amidst much laughter as the two guards passed the bottle between them, back and forth until it was gone.

"Hey! Whose birthday is this?" Jaroslav protested as the empty bottle was handed back to him with a raucous laugh.

"Happy birthday to you, young fellow! And give our respects to your wife." The guards let them through without a second glance at Zdenek and after an interminable length of time he let out a huge sigh of relief. He was home.

The year was 1988. Who was to know that Czechoslovakia would be free by 1989?

Zdenek travelled only as far as the nearest village and took leave of his saviours with many thanks on his part and much well wishing on theirs.

Zdenek's plan was to remain anonymous. He did not want trouble for his family and he was not going to take any chances. He could never have foreseen the effect this would have on his mind.

He made his way to a small town east of Kosice, called Michalovce, and there holed himself in, lost to everyone he knew and loved and gradually to himself as well.

Freedom came for Czechoslovakia and the Czechs split amicably with Slovakia, but somehow Zdenek did not seem to know. He remained in Slovakia, sunk into a condition brought on by guilt and regret for the pain he believed he had caused his family. Remorse did not allow him to raise his head and see the light. Deep inside was the clear knowledge that he had a daughter lost in Canada, and a mother and brother from whom he was hiding. Someday, he knew, the time would arrive when he would be able to reunite with them. Until that day came he would remain wrapped within himself.

So time passed, and if it were possible for a man to become the lost and deprived person he had set out to become, then Zdenek Velkovsky became that man. He was quiet and unassuming, well liked by his co-workers at the small plant where he carved beautiful furniture for the up-and-coming would-be elites of the brand new Republics of Czech and Slovakia. He was known as Tomas Havlik.

"Then, he's alive!" Dali was beside himself with joy. "And he's in Slovakia."

"Yes, he is alive, but . . . ."

"But what?" Dali said. "It doesn't matter if he is ill, or . . . different. He is my brother. I have to go to him."

Robert sat forward now, keenly aware that something else was coming. "Jan, what else are you trying to say?" Jan looked at Robert gratefully.

"I think that Zdenek does not want to see his family," he said softly. "He has denied that he has a family. He cannot bear to look back on the past. The punishment he received from the State served to convince him that he is at fault for the destruction of his family's happiness."

"Are you saying he has lost his mind?" Robert asked directly.

"I would rather say his mind is buried so deep that it cannot be easily found."

"Where is he?" demanded Dali, his face white and grim.

"I can take you to him," Jan said, studying Dali carefully.

"When?"

"As soon as we can be ready. It is a day's drive from here to Michalovce. Are you prepared for a few days stay? It would be sensible to leave early tomorrow morning rather than immediately." Dali calmed down enough to see the sense of this and agreed that it would be wise to drive the half hour back to Stramberk and pack a small case.

"But what about Zdenek's mother and little Myshka?" Jan said. "I do not think it would be wise for them or Zdenek to meet so suddenly. It could be so bitterly disappointing."

"I disagree!" said Dalibor. "We have all waited too long for this day. Why prolong the agony. And besides, you will realise that 'Little Myshka' is no longer so little." And with that, Dali and Rob took their leave with the understanding that they would return with Michaela and his mother by eight o'clock the next morning. Rob took the time to phone school to arrange a few extra days leave of absence, needed, he explained, for a family crisis.

The Czech Republic

Ofelia was waiting with perfect confidence for Dali and Robert to return. She sat happily with her "Babichka", who was regaling her with stories about her father. There is nothing so revealing about a mother's love for a grown son than watching her remember his childhood, and to see the exchange was to know in your bones, that like Christmas with all the sparkle and glitter, this man would soon be here.

Edda was kept busy e-mailing the folks back home with updates. Even Ofelia found time to put in a long conversation to her parents. She reassured them of her love and intention to return shortly, but first she hoped for the longed for reunion with her birth father. Dali and Robert returned bearing the news that Zdenek was alive, but possibly not well. There was no hesitation. The Velkovsky women were packed and ready in a trice.

"Let's go now!" pealed through the air in two languages.

Slovakia

Tomas Havlik was at work earlier than usual after another night of broken dreams. To work was to fill the mind. It prevented the mud from filtering up from the past. Half the night he had been battling with these dark shadows. As a result, here he was trying to chisel a pattern into a piece of wood for the back of a chair, on a dark November morning when he should still be in bed. On top of that, it was not working. The constant image of his little girl with uplifted arms and tears streaming down her face all those years ago in Canada would not go. *Tati! Tati!* Would that voice, which he had successfully kept at bay for years now, never leave him alone? He found tears on his own face. He had literally carved himself a life in this town, with no past. He had made himself into a mild and likeable man. This was his penance and atonement. He would never see his family again.

This decision of the earlier Zdenek Velkovsky had been won with heavy consequences. The self-flagellation of the early Church martyrs could not have had better results. He had beaten down his painful memories so well that they were macerated beyond recognition. But lately, some demon had been down there moulding them back together again. He found that the pain was worse than before.

An hour later the arrival of the other workers to begin the day helped Tomas pull himself together, and he managed to bring his hard-earned good will to the surface. He thought he had it all under control, but his boss came to him and told him to take the afternoon off.

"You do better work when you sleep longer Tomu." Tomas went home. He was sitting irresolutely at the table in his one room flat looking out over the dreary November garden when there was a ring on his doorbell. He felt a flash of annoyance. *Why could they never leave him alone?* His kindness had made him many friends who found reasons to call just to say hello, bring him a gift or ask for a favour. Normally he was grateful, but with this battle going on inside, he felt he was fighting for sanity. He flung his chair back and went out into the small hallway to open his door.

A stranger stood there, a young woman of about twenty-five years who somehow reminded him of his wife, of Katya. *More foolishness!* She started to speak,

"I . . ." Then, to his consternation, she began to fall. She must have felt faint. Her hands reached out to catch herself. He grasped those hands and instinctively drew her into his home and through to the one comfortable chair by the fire.

"Sit down!" he told her in Slovak, and fetched a glass of water.

"Ne mluvim Cesky," she said in Czech. *I don't speak Czech.* He noted she was American by her accent.

"Canada!" She seemed to respond to his thought. He froze. The girl looked at him. She seemed unable to continue.

"I speak English," he said, unsurely. Ofelia, for it was of course she, knew he had very little English; probably as much English as she had Czech. Between them however they might have enough for the job in hand.

"My name is Ofelia," she began.

"Tomas Havlik," he said, offering his hand. She stared at him and shook her head.

"Tomas Havlik," he repeated, fear rising. There was a small silence. She pointed at him and said with a question in her voice

"Tomas?" Then she pointed at herself and shaking her head vehemently in the negative, she said,

"*Ja ne ysem Ofelia.* I am not Ofelia."

Again the silence. She sipped at the water, not looking at this man who was her father. He stalked around his kitchen while she tried to unravel the difference between the Czech word for remember and forget, these being the words she needed to tell her father that she had not forgotten him, that she still remembered him. The word was tied up in the Czech language with the word "memory", and it was important to get it right. Nothing came to mind. Meanwhile, his thoughts were bent on a different track. He strode up and down in his kitchen trying to remember the words to a popular Czech song of his day. If he could just put the verse together he could stave up his slowly crumbling fortifications. He fully believed that he could not deal with extra torture on the subject of the family he had so wronged. *This was a trick to break him. Who was out there today that would still want his downfall after his twenty years of freedom?* Ofelia's mind had become a blank. She stared, distraught at the pacing man. She was the one who had insisted on coming in alone to meet him.

Into Tomas's mind a small thought was pushing its way persistently upward. *Look for the birthmark!* He sat down opposite the girl and quietly took her left hand in his. Turning it palm up and pushing her sleeve up, he found the much faded red crescent moon, the size of a small coin. His mind stilled. He dared not move a single particle of himself. He waited. Into the stillness crept a memory of his wife and himself cradling their newborn daughter and delighting in her perfection. The little red mark marred nothing of her beauty. They had named her Michaela, after the great Arch Angel Michael, the "Beloved of God".

"Zdenek? Tati?" she said timidly. She rose from the chair, and clasped her hands together at her throat. It was a plea for acceptance. The dam burst and Zdenek stood and in one step, clasped her against his heart.

"My baby? My Myshka!" Never had there been so many tears of joy and pain relieved and running like a river, washing away the sickness of Zdenek's perception of truth and drenching Ofelia's longing and loneliness until her old name was quite washed away and she knew she was truly Michaela. She was whole again.

Some time later they went to the door and looked up the path towards town. They saw three people approaching; Dalibor, his mother Elishka and Robert Halley a step or two behind, present on Dalibor's insistence, as an independent witness.

Tomas Havlik was receding gently and the returning Zdenek, still bruised and half comatose, saw first his mother, older, much older, hurrying in slow motion, sending the same glad smile with which she had always welcomed him. He hurried dreamlike towards her too. It took forever to close the gap but it was just thirty long seconds before he held her gently in his arms and she sobbed against his chest.

"I thought you were dead. Forgive me! I thought you were dead," she cried.

Dali came and put his arms around them both. They remained so for a while. Michaela, who had held back for them, felt that there was nothing left to wish for in this world. Robert had come round to her side and held her hand in empathy. She smiled up at him.

Michaela's happiness was complete.

The Quest was over.

What Next?

The whole party drove back together to Stramberk. Edda and George were waiting along with Vera and Petr, dying to know how it all went.

Zdenek's hand was wrung and wrung. Even the neighbours came in. He had given notice to his employer back in Michalovce and now he was home in Stramberk as Zdenek Velkovsky.

Dalibor decided he could instruct skiers and organise mountain hikes equally well from the Beskydy Hills of home as from the high Tatras in Slovakia. He too would come home to live.

Ofelia, now officially Michaela, had decided to stay on at least until after Christmas.

Elishka's delight was tangible.

E-mails and phone calls to Canada spread the news of the success of the Quest.

The Velkovskys cordially invited all of Michaela's adoptive family to come and spend Christmas with them in Stramberk. The invitation was extended to Edda and George. George chose to decline as he was looking forward to being back with his own family, but promised to be on web cam for a Christmas conversation. Edda further extended a special invitation to Cleo as she had had such a hand in the original encouragement of the Quest.

Besides, Edda thought, Cleo *needed a break from her husband.*

Elizabeth and Stan Kingsley, cancelled their trip to Mexico and booked for Europe instead. Dave and Ed, Elizabeth's sons from her first marriage, were delighted to be asked and accepted with alacrity.

Dave and Anthea were secretly thrilled to be taking a holiday together in this unexpected way. And upon discussion it was discovered that they had both always wanted to see Prague.

"It would be lovely to see Prague with you." Anthea said daringly.

And then Cleo's husband put the cat among the pigeons by stating that he also would like to come with them.

"What am I going to do?" Cleo desperately asked of Edda, inappropriately telephoning and awakening the Novak household at around midnight. "He'd be the death of any joyful celebration." She moaned pitifully, quite unlike her usual self. Edda was concerned but groggy.

"Look, Cleo! Give him a chance. What has made him want to come with us anyway?" she asked sleepily. "I've always assumed he had no time for wasting on this sort of jaunt."

"He never has before," Cleo said. "I don't know what's got into him and I don't know what to do. I suppose when he realised that I was taking off to some obscure middle European Eastern Bloc country for the holidays, he thought he had to do something about it." Edda, who was dying to get back to bed, said,

"You've just got to talk to him. Find out why. Call me back in the morning and I'll help you think of something if you are still stuck."

"Oh! Sorry Edda! Sorry! I didn't think of the time difference. I woke you up! Oh Edda! You're a pal. Go back to sleep. I'll deal with it and call you back at a decent hour. Bye." Cleo put the phone down quickly and went to face the music.

William was in his study. He was watching a program on finance on his own TV. They never watched TV together.

"Why do you always watch on your own in here?" she started. He stood up, switched it off and did not answer. They each sat down. They both knew there was some kind of a showdown coming. William spoke first.

"Do you remember when we first met, how you used to break into song when we were out walking together or when you were working about the hotel?" Cleo nodded.

"I remember what a free spirit you were, so young and lively and full of fun. You were the best thing that ever happened to me." Cleo's eyebrows lifted just a fraction.

"Where has that girl gone?" he asked.

"That was fifteen years ago," she said.

"You know what I mean," he stated, looking at her steadfastly, willing her to tell him the truth about himself and hoping he could take it.

"I have *my* version," she said.

"Tell me."

"Back home," she said, taking her courage in both hands, "you led me to believe that you loved me, thought me beautiful, intelligent and someone you wanted to spend your life with. The truth is, after you were back in Canada, you remembered that all women are fools and that you had been led astray by island magic." There! She had begun. "On top of that," she continued, "you couldn't bear to see me escape from your thrall and become independent by using the intelligence that I am not supposed to possess. You could hardly believe that I might actually be as successful as you are. You are in fact threatened by me and now you think you can come along to the Czech Republic and find out what it is about me that you have missed. Well, let me tell you, you have missed everything because you live with your head buried in a very small hole and you are letting life pass you by because of it. I may be your wife but I won't be buried with you and I do *not* want your shitty attitude with me for Christmas. So you are *not* coming with me."

William was silenced. He had heard the worst and it was no better than he had expected. He wondered if it was in his power to rectify anything. It would be a mistake to tell her that he loved her at this juncture even though it was true.

"Do you think I was lying to you fifteen years ago on the Island?"

"No, I think you are lying to yourself here about the false kind of life you live."

"Are you saying that my life is a lie?" he asked incredulously.

"Yes, I am really."

"Can you help me change that?" he asked quietly. Cleo looked stunned as well she might. William had never before given her cause to hope for such a miracle.

"I don't know," she said truthfully.

"In my heart," William said, "I am still the same person that you knew in Trinidad. You are right. There *was* some island magic but you were the greater part of it. And when we returned I was not able to overcome my fear of failure and reverted to the safety of my old self."

"What fear of failure are you talking about?" Cleo asked, puzzled.

"The fear of not being important," he said shamefacedly. Cleo suppressed a giggle. Then she gave what he had said some thought.

"You were afraid of not being an important person?"

He nodded.

"So you made yourself a success in business in order to be important?" she confirmed. He nodded again.

"But where are your feelings of love and compassion and kindness?" she stormed. "Don't you want to be loved yourself?" Enlightenment dawned.

"You think you only want to be loved by important people!" she said.

"I want to be loved by you," he said, trying not to look stricken.

"Are you sure?" Cleo said. She possessed a large and generous nature.

"Very sure," he said. Cleo stood up, went to him, and sat on his lap.

"How sure?" she asked.

Part III

Christmas in the Czech Republic

Edda flew back to Toronto one week after George. She had been asked by her old school if she would like to return and teach in January. She had accepted with alacrity and so would be returning to the Czech Republic on December the 23rd. To be there for Christmas was a treat Edda had long wanted to experience. Cleo had phoned and cleared that she would like to bring William. She assured Edda most enigmatically that it was her own wish that he accompany her. They were to travel on the same flight with the Kingsleys and Ed Nelson. Anthea and Dave had gone on ahead on an earlier flight to spend a couple of days alone in Prague. They found a small hotel where they decided to share a room, as the cost was rather more than they had expected to pay. They took a twin bedded room because after all, they were good friends and mature enough to sleep in the same room in separate beds. However somehow they ended up in the same bed with a great deal of satisfaction on both sides. They discovered both the wonders of the city and of each other. They had an electrifying time.

And further, while they were watching the hour strike on the old clock in Stary Mesto, a pickpocket tried to make off with Anthea's purse. Dave tripped the thief and grabbed the purse back. Dave was fast becoming a hero in Anthea's eyes.

They caught a bus to Ruzyne Airport to meet Dave's parents and brother and the rest of the group, and subsequently all travelled together in the express train that took them from Prague to Ostrava in double quick time compared to the usual slow old corridor train that Edda was used to, and rather preferred. And yes, William was with them. What a charming man he turned out to be! He and Cleo behaved like newlyweds and Anthea and Dave were clearly love struck. Elizabeth and Stan Kingsley felt a little out of place but were obviously mightily impressed and Edda promised them a day in Prague before they flew home.

Two cars driven by Robert and Dalibor met them in Ostrava and the group was squeezed in for the short ride to Stramberk where a warm welcome awaited them. Dusk was falling and the little town was lit up for the season. The medieval wooden houses of Stramberk and its old "Tube" tower lit the whole sky as they drove into town. The Velkovsky brothers had rented what was tantamount to a villa by Czech standards and it was situated on the lower levels of the little town so they had a driveway and parking for the cars. It was a grand house with several bedrooms and a couple of bathrooms, and Elishka had done herself proud with preparations, skipping between her own small home and the kitchen of her sons' new place. Dalibor had bought two large carp fish, which were swimming in one of the bathtubs.

"Tomas and Ofelia!" He named them proudly. "We will eat them on Christmas Eve." Elizabeth Kingsley nearly fainted.

"Czech tradition," said her erstwhile daughter, smiling cheerfully and taking Elizabeth back downstairs to introduce her properly to Robert. Elizabeth and Stan had both been wondering at the young Canadian in their midst. No one had explained his presence and now Michaela told the story of the part he had played in the quest. Elizabeth was dumbfounded and shook the young man warmly by the hand. She could see quite clearly the powerful connection between the two and she was pleased. In fact, Elizabeth was enjoying the whole experience. She was proud of her adopted daughter's persistence and courage, and how it had paid off. Her own experience at her daughter's age had required a different kind of bravery. She had been widowed at the age of twenty-six with two small boys with a third child on the way. She had come through it and four years later had met and married Stan. They had decided to come to Canada, seeing it as a land of opportunity. Stan had generously and heartily accepted her three sons as his own and a few years later they had adopted young Mary Morton and taken her to their hearts. They had never regretted this but when Ofelia, as she had renamed herself, began to search for her true identity, Elizabeth had suffered pangs of jealousy that she found hard to overcome. Now, she had no doubt that it had all been for the best, and if anything, Ofelia's love for her adoptive parents seemed even greater.

"I told you so," Stan had told her. "You need never have doubted Ofelia's love for us. She's true blue. I'm only surprised she didn't originate from Old Blighty!"

"Oh Stan!" she had answered, her woe turning to laughter, "you are such a pain and a comfort." But her mind turned inevitably to her almost estranged son Richard in England. *If only he could be here to share with them now.*

At this precise moment, Stan was learning the art of tossing back Slivovitz, and a good job he was making of it too. Zdenek, who drank rarely, and on this occasion only to celebrate their wonderful fortune, studied Stan and saw that he was a good man. How lucky that such a man had been able to protect his little girl as she grew up. He thanked the stars that his Myshka had been blessed with a loving family. Michaela and Elizabeth entered the room with Robert and joined the others, who were standing around and despite their exhaustion, still desiring to communicate. Elizabeth went to her husband's side, Michaela to his other side between him and her newly found father, Zdenek.

Stan and Zden, how strangely alike they sounded, she thought. Across the circle Robert's eyes locked with hers and a smile curved both their lips. Her grandmother beamed at her fondly and with the enormous satisfaction of knowing she could not have wished for anything greater than to see her family united again like this.

After that it was an early night for them all. The travellers were tired and the language difficulties too great a challenge on this first day. The morning would bring new sharing.

Christmas Eve 2008 arrived. It was a day they would never forget as long as they lived. Petr and Vera had joined them for an hour or two before joining their own families, and when darkness fell everyone sat around the fire exchanging small gifts, and small talk. The interpreting that had gone on for most of the day had unearthed their deep caring and love and there was the feeling that everything had been satisfactorily brought to completion.

Zdenek, perhaps most of all, had emerged out of his years of pain and forgiven himself. He knew now that his Myshka had been well loved and had wonderful friends. He was thankful for her Canadian parents and his appreciation of them was ceaseless, and they in turn were gratified that their Mary-Ofelia-Michaela should have found such a blessing in her biological father and her new family. They and most of their party found the stories of life in Czechoslovakia twenty years ago difficult to imagine, and William in particular paid close attention to them.

Dalibor was amazed at the amount of "coincidence" that had brought them all together. Right down to the fact that Edda had taught English to Vera, who turned out to be the link with the Velkovskys through Petr. Zdenek and he both confessed to strong feelings when bringing the past, that they had tried to keep buried for years, to the surface. Michaela said it had all started on that Saturday on her way to market when she met Anthea for the first time and Anthea had sent her to meet Edda who had recognised the shield of Novy Jicin on her old shawl. Elishka beamed. *Incredible! Incredible!*

"And then," Michaela reminded them, "Edda had become all excited and said that we simply had to travel on a quest to reunite me with my lost father. And we immediately started the preparations. George insisted on joining us too."

Here Anthea chipped in with the fact that she had thought her mother had gone mad. They all laughed. Then Zdenek spoke.

"It was in November that I started to get disturbed with memories of when I sent Michaela to the safety of Canada. I too thought that I was going mad." His eyes were fixed on Edda. *The connections were more than coincidence.*

Edda looked at him and wondered at how this man moved her. Zdenek smiled at her.

"And Robert, remember the night in the wood when we were lost and we had that remarkable experience with time?" asked Dali.

"That was not coincidence," Robert said. "That was the working of something more powerful than ourselves."

"Yes!" said Michaela. "That was the answer to my prayers. You were both kept safe." Robert studied her face.

"You didn't know I existed then," he said.

"I must have done," she said as if that were an end to it.

Cleo and William held hands, watching the evening unfold. Cleo was thinking of Ann and George. They had returned from France a few weeks ago, bubbling with happiness and then George, by some stroke of the same serendipity was offered a position at the University of Guelph managing the arrival of incoming international students. His job was to welcome them to the country and see that they found accommodations and people to help them through all their initial difficulties, and also to provide an ongoing support system for when they needed it. He was given a small team of workers to help him, a fairly generous expense allowance and a decent salary. The magical shawl had covered him as well.

Now, here was the party celebrating the wonderful quest that had touched them all and given far more than expected. They had eaten and enjoyed the carp and now very soon midnight would be striking.

Dalibor filled their glasses once more and they all stood when the churches of Stramberk started to peal.

"To love, faith and courage!" he said gloriously, his glass held high. They all raised their glasses.

"To love, faith and courage" echoed in Czech and English. Then to the surprise of the Canadians, they trooped outside in the snow to briefly toast any neighbours who were doing the same thing.

"Happy Christmas" rang through the midnight air. "Vesele Vanoce!"

Back in the living room the fire was dying and they started wending their way bedwards with a lot of kissing and hugging to help it on. Soon just Robert and Michaela were left sitting close together on the couch. Robert smiled meditatively at Michaela, who sat idly fingering her grandmother's shawl. He stroked her cheek then picked up his guitar, on which he had been playing Christmas carols earlier.

"I have one more song to sing before we take ourselves off to bed," he said, and plucking a chord, he began.

> *When you come to the end of a perfect day,*
> *And you sit alone with your thought,*
> *When the chimes ring out with a carol gay*
> *For the joy that the day has brought.*
> *Have you thought what the end of a perfect day*
> *Can mean to a tired heart,*
> *When the sun goes down with a flaming ray*
> *And the dear friends have to part.*

Well, this is the end of a perfect day,
Near the end of a journey too.
But it leaves a wish that is big and strong
With a thought that is kind and true.
For love has painted this perfect day,
With colours that never fade.
And you find at the end of a perfect day,
The soul of a friend you've made."

The End